"I've never been divorced," she blurted out. *"Or married. Or engaged. Or even very serious."*

"You strike me as *very* serious."

"About a man. Was what I meant."

"I'm teasing you, Rowena." She felt foolish until Ben added, "Because if I don't undercut your advantage a little, I am about to make myself very, very emotionally naked, telling a virtual stranger what went wrong with my marriage."

"Oh, please don't feel you have to do that!" She pressed a hand to her cheek, stricken at the fact that she seemed to have drawn out a vulnerable side to Ben Radford that she wouldn't have thought could exist.

He was still smiling at her, in his cynical, smokey-eyed and almost dangerous way, and all at once it was too much. It seemed more like flirting than anything else, and Dr. Rowena Madison just did not *do* flirting.

She didn't know how.

And she didn't want to learn.

Dear Reader,

In March 2007 I spent a great week in San Diego attending a writing conference and researching this book. Fabulous Harlequin Presents author and friend Jane Porter and I went on a day tour that took in missions, wineries and beautiful Southern California scenery. It's always hard to pinpoint how research works its way into a book, but our day and my whole week are there in the detail of the sounds, smells, sights and atmosphere of this beautiful part of the world.

At least, I'm hoping it's still beautiful. I was shocked to hear of the region's devastating fires last fall, and can't help wondering how my hero's ranch fared. I imagine him chartering his own helicopters to drop thousands of gallons of water in order to save his cattle and protect his beloved home. The thing about wildfires is that nature heals the damage faster than you'd expect. We had our own terrible fires here several years ago, but now the trees are growing back, the bird and animal life has returned and people have rebuilt their homes. The great part about writing fiction, however, is that I can have everything turn out exactly the way I want, so I'm here to tell you that Ben's ranch didn't burn and it's still just as beautiful as you'll find it in this book.

Lilian Darcy

THE MILLIONAIRE'S MAKEOVER

LILIAN DARCY

SPECIAL EDITION

Published by Silhouette Books

America's Publisher of Contemporary Romance

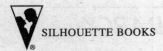

SILHOUETTE BOOKS

ISBN-13: 978-0-373-24899-5
ISBN-10:   0-373-24899-7

THE MILLIONAIRE'S MAKEOVER

Printed in U.S.A.

2502547

Books by Lilian Darcy

Silhouette Special Edition

Balancing Act #1552
Their Baby Miracle #1672
The Father Factor #1696
†*The Runaway and
    the Cattleman* #1762
†*Princess in Disguise* #1766
†*Outback Baby* #1774
The Couple Most Likely To #1801
A Mother in the Making #1880
The Millionaire's Makeover #1899

Silhouette Romance

The Baby Bond #1390
Her Sister's Child #1449
Raising Baby Jane #1478
*Cinderella After Midnight #1542
*Saving Cinderella #1555
*Finding Her Prince #1567
Pregnant and Protected #1603
For the Taking #1620
The Boss's Baby Surprise #1729
*The Millionaire's
    Cinderella Wife* #1772
Sister Swap #1816

†Wanted: Outback Wives
*The Cinderella Conspiracy

LILIAN DARCY

has written more than seventy-five books for Silhouette Romance, Special Edition and Harlequin Medical Romance (Prescription Romance) Her first novel for Silhouette Books appeared on the Waldenbooks series romance bestsellers list, and she's hoping readers go on responding strongly to her work. Happily married, with four active children, she enjoys keeping busy and could probably fill several more lifetimes with the things she likes to do—including cooking, gardening, quilting, drawing and traveling. She currently lives in Australia but travels to the United States as often as possible to visit family. Lilian loves to hear from readers. You can write to her at: P.O. Box 532 Jamison P.O., Macquarie ACT 2614, Australia, or e-mail her at: lilian@liliandarcy.com.

Chapter One

Rowena gritted her teeth and held her clipboard more tightly, as if attempting to get a literal and physical grip on her fast-disappearing patience. "And one final question…" she said.

"Final? Really? Thank heaven for small mercies," muttered the man who stood beside her.

Without so much as a glance in her direction, he reached into the inner jacket pocket of his perfectly tailored business suit and brought out a cell phone. Apparently empires might crumble if he didn't have it pressed to his ear within three seconds.

And apparently he'd already dismissed Rowena as the slightly prim, conservatively dressed, uninteresting academic type that she was—which, actually, she was quite comfortable being most of the time—and didn't look at her for long enough to revise this impression. His steely gaze missed the region of her face by at least two yards.

She ignored his rudeness and persisted, "Do you like barbecues?"

"Do I like *what?*"

"Um, when you have friends over, there are salads and beer, you cook outside on a grill…? Bar-be-cues," she articulated clearly and helpfully, as if speaking to someone who'd begun learning English yesterday.

"I know what barbecues are, Dr. Madison." He favored her with a quarter-second gaze, at last. "Listen, I'm a very busy man—"

"Yes, and you're exactly the kind of man I don't like," she cut in. The words spilled out before she'd consciously decided to speak them. Her tone sliced into the balmy Southern California air like an icicle splintering onto a concrete driveway. "I understand very well that you're busy. And seriously, *radioactively* important. And that I'm not. Please don't feel that you have to *parade* the fact, with your cell phone as a prop, in order to get it through to me. I'm not stupid, and I don't appreciate being treated that way."

Feeling the angry heat creep into her cheeks, she threw the clipboard onto an ancient wooden workbench that had been abandoned for no discernible reason on the adobe brick veranda. The clipboard's attached pages, covered in her neat blue handwriting, fluttered. Ben Radford dropped his cell phone into his trouser pocket in surprise at her frank speaking and took a shocked step back.

The mouse had roared. Who knew?

His reaction almost made Rowena laugh out loud. His well-shaped mouth had fallen open and then snapped shut again. He was wiping the back of his neck with his lean fingers as if he'd begun to itch or sweat. He was sinfully good-looking and dressed for unquestioning success, and there was something quite shocking about seeing him out of his depth, even for a few seconds.

Should she try harder to choke back her anger, she wondered, or make this potential client aware of exactly how she felt? Roar some more or creep back into her warm, familiar mouse hole?

She went with her gut.

"You've bought this historic, exceptional, wonderful place," she said. "Spent twenty million on it, I should think. You've asked me to consult with you on the restoration of its garden, and as you know, my rates are commensurate with my expertise. High, in other words."

Don't splutter, Row, she coached herself. *Stick to the point. Believe in yourself. You're in the right.*

"All I'm doing," she went on, "is attempting to gauge your priorities, your budget, your needs and your concerns. How important is historical accuracy? How do you plan to actually use the garden? What is your wish list of features? How much do you want to spend? Those are not trivial issues, and yet you have made it painfully apparent from the first minute of our meeting that I'm an irritant, and that you have more important things to do."

"Dr. Madison—"

"May I remind you that you arranged my visit here today. If a fantastic opportunity such as the one presented by this property is no more than an afterthought to you, I do have to wonder why on earth you're proposing to employ me. Why not get on the phone, get a bulldozer in and order a bulk delivery of geraniums and precut turf instead!"

She snatched her clipboard up from the ancient bench. Actually, the bench was so ancient that it might be worth keeping as an antique. Not that she'd be a part of such decisions now, after such a frank expression of her attitude.

Was she sorry that she'd said so much?

She pondered the question as she snapped her way over the worn adobe in her neat, sensible shoes, her unbuttoned tailored jacket flapping open at the front like two gray bird's wings and the black fabric of her synthetic-blend trouser legs catching at her calves and generating megawatts of static cling, thanks to her haste.

There was no point in going back through the magnificently restored house. She could take the side exit from this overgrown mission-style courtyard and proceed directly to her car. She would invoice Ben Radford for her travel expenses today, regard their short-lived business relationship as over, and, just by the way, she would never wear these horrible, clingy trousers again.

No, she decided, she wasn't sorry that she'd spoken the way she had. She'd defended both her own professional worth and the worth of Mr. Radford's neglected and unloved piece of ground, and she was proud of having spoken her mind.

It was a huge personal milestone, and her whole body still tingled with the triumph of having reached it.

Two years earlier she would have burst into speechless tears, paralyzed by the very thought of a confrontation with a forbiddingly arrogant and successful man like this, no matter how much justice was on her side.

She would have rushed home to hide and not answered the phone for a week, in case it was Mr. Radford calling. She'd have relived the encounter over and over, exaggerating it in her memory until it froze her completely and stopped her from leaving the safety of her home.

This time she'd actually said what she really thought.

She felt a little dizzy, bubbling over with the need to share the victory and to celebrate it somehow. Putting the clingy trousers into a charity rag bin wouldn't be celebration enough. She decided to call Rox—her identical twin—with a full report as soon as she could. Rox would probably send her champagne.

Losing the chance to work on such a fabulous garden restoration gave her some regrets, true, but it couldn't be helped. If Ben Radford was this difficult to deal with at their first consultation, he'd be a nightmare further down the track. She should consider this as a lucky escape.

"Wait a minute, Dr. Madison!" he said beside her, just as she was about to push on the rusty iron gate that led out of the courtyard.

She hadn't realized he'd followed her. He studied her in silence for a long moment, as if deciding how she should be handled. Bomb-disposal experts and pest exterminators probably studied suspiciously ticking packages and enormous wasp nests in the same way. "You're being too hasty," he said at last.

"I wasn't the one rushing us through the consultation."

"No, but you're the one bailing out now."

"With good reason. This project has to mean something to you, or there's no point in hiring me." Sheesh, she was going all out today! She'd had no idea it could feel so good. She lifted her chin and stared him down.

To be met with a silence that stretched and stretched.

"You got me at a bad moment," he said abruptly at last, his dark eyes half-hidden by lowered lids. "I'm sorry." He sounded seriously uncomfortable, and Rowena guessed that he hadn't felt the need to apologize for anything in a long time. She had the strong suspicion this was because he very rarely did anything wrong. "You're right, you are a professional. And this project is important to me."

"Okay, good," she murmured vaguely, not knowing how else to respond to such a surprising admission from such a man. Then some devilish part of her that she barely knew existed added, "I hope there's more."

"More?"

"More to your excuse." She dared a smile. "How often might I expect these bad moments, if you contract me for the project?"

Since she was by now quite certain that he wouldn't, it didn't matter if she burned her boats. Meanwhile, the satisfying sense of having shattered her past limitations hadn't yet begun to fade. It was probably the closest she was ever going to get to jumping out of an airplane and going into free fall with a parachute on her back.

"I was on the phone with my ex-wife just before you arrived," Ben Radford said slowly, "and it was a miserable conversation, as usual. Is that good enough? Divorce is stressful." He said the *D* word as if he was never going to get used to the bad taste it left in his mouth. "But I shouldn't have taken it out on you. That was wrong of me."

His expression remained wooden, distant and severe, which somehow showed his unhappiness more clearly than a grimace of misery would have done.

He continued. "And you're quite right about any garden designer's need to know my priorities and tastes if this project is going to be done the way it should be. So can we start again?"

He gave a tight, suffering smile, and something kicked in Rowena's stomach. The man was tall, well built, dark-haired, good-looking, and she guessed he could have a great deal of personal charm if he ever chose to use it. Evidently, he wasn't quite ready to use it now.

Still, he had apologized at manful length, she had to concede.

Then realized, good grief, that she was almost disappointed about the concessions he'd just made. What was happening to her? She would have very much liked a good excuse to do some more yelling. It felt…so exhilarating.

Suppressing such an inappropriate emotion, she said a little awkwardly, "We don't need to start again. I've already taken pages of notes."

"That's not what I meant." He smiled again, dark eyes smoky, charm level rising, vulnerability totally gone, hair catching the morning sunlight for a moment as he lifted his head, and this time the kick in her stomach was stronger and held a warning.

Stay cool, Rowena...

A familiar impulse to run and hide began to well up inside her, but she fought it down. She could handle this. Handle *him*. His charm, his eyes, his wealth, his unsettling moment of honesty about his divorce, the whole package.

And if she couldn't totally handle it, yet, then she had to practice and learn.

"Back to the barbecue question, then," she said lightly, smoothing down the lapels of her jacket. "Could I have an answer?"

He rested his hand on the rusted wrought iron of the gate and surveyed the courtyard. A frown tightened on his brow. He didn't look like an Englishman, with those dark eyes and the natural olive tint to his skin. He didn't even sound like one, some of the time. He'd been in Southern California for a while, and he had the American vowels to prove it. But Rowena knew that he had come from England, originally, because she'd looked him up on the Internet.

He'd come from a comfortable, classy background and had attended a very expensive school. He'd earned two degrees at Oxford University and married an American bride. He'd made his fortune in the field of biotechnology, sold his company a year ago and moved into new and more-varied business interests. He now owned an art gallery, a Hollywood casting agency and a restaurant, amongst other things.

The Internet hadn't told Rowena that he was in the middle of an obviously unpleasant divorce.

"I wish I could tell you," he murmured.

"You don't know whether you like barbecues?"

"I don't know whether my liking for the occasional barbecue means we should build a barbecue in this courtyard, if that's what you're trying to work out. Look at it!" He gestured at the wild, intimidating jungle in front of them, sounding…daunted? Surely not. He didn't look like the kind of man who could be daunted by anything. "I'm fascinated by the idea of restoring the place, but can't begin to imagine how it will work."

"That's why you're considering the possibility of hiring me," she reminded him.

They both stood in silence, contemplating the sprawling space. It was bracketed at one end by the three sides of the old adobe ranch house, already well on its way to being a showpiece thanks to the injection of Ben Radford's money and effort.

He was still in the process of restoration, but the rooms that were already finished were spectacular without being overdone, and with a personal touch that had spoken to Rowena immediately as she'd passed through them. Clean lines, unexpected colors, well-chosen antiques, pockets of warmth and coziness that made you want to curl up in them with a good book.

The contrast between the yard and the house was almost shocking.

Barring one or two dusty pathways, the entire expanse— well over an acre—was a towering tangle of cactus, some of it probably a hundred years old. Rowena had identified prickly pear, several species of agave, ocotillo, barrel cactus and half a dozen other species. The plants twisted together like some bizarre maze. Dead husks rattled on the ground, painful spines reached out to snag the unwary. There would be birds' nests in there, insects of all kinds and snakes…

"You mentioned bulldozers a minute ago," Ben Radford said. His voice held a thoughtful note.

They were both standing quite still. San Diego, Oceanside and La Jolla were each less than an hour's drive away, along with the urban sprawl that marched farther in from the ocean year by year. Here, beyond the vineyards and nursery plantations closer to the coast, the old Spanish-land-grant ranch sat poised at the foot of the mountains, surrounded by air you could really breathe. The house seemed more a part of the earth than a human creation. There were cattle grazing in the distance and horses inhabiting the old stables, and it was very peaceful.

"I wasn't serious," Rowena said quickly.

"Why not?" He frowned at her. He wasn't the kind of man to accept setbacks or contradictory opinions.

"Because we don't know what's beneath all this," she explained, knowing she wouldn't have much opportunity to convince him. "It would be a crime to come in with heavy machinery. There could be a treasure trove destroyed in the process. Old household items that would belong in a museum, and heirloom plant strains that might be very hard to find now. Do you see these powdery silver-white patches on the prickly pear?"

"They look like damp erupting behind whitewash in a mildewed basement," he said.

"They do, but take a bit of it and crush it in your fingers."

He reached out and did so, then looked up at her in astonishment at the brilliant crimson red that had stained his skin. "That's amazing. What is it?"

"Cochineal. Those white patches are colonies of living creatures—a kind of scale insect. They store the red pigment in their bodies. Before the Spanish arrived in Mexico, the Mixtec Indians farmed these insects on the cactus and used them to make dye. There were periods when it was almost as precious as gold. It was used as a food coloring, too, for a long time, in jams, medicines, candy."

"I've heard of it."

"You've probably eaten it."

"That's fascinating."

"This might sound strange," Rowena went on slowly, "but I have a feeling that the whole garden could provide the same experience as you've just had with the cochineal. Nothing to get excited about at first glance, but if you take a closer look, if you approach with delicacy, you discover its magic. I'd hate to bring in a bulldozer, Mr. Radford—"

"Call me Ben," he ordered. "I won't need to tell you that again, I hope."

"Ben," she repeated, and that warning *thunk* hit her stomach again, more powerfully than ever. Why did she like the idea of calling him Ben? "Um, I hope you won't. And, uh, Rowena, for me. Or Rowie." Why had she added that? It was the nickname her sister called her by, and sometimes Mom and Dad. A client had no need to know it.

He was still looking at the crimson stain on his fingertips, and he had incredible hands—strong and lean and smooth. Sure hands, the way almost everything about him seemed sure.

Oh, except for that one very telling moment when he'd mentioned his divorce.

She could smell the aura of soap and coffee and clean male skin that hovered around him and it did something to her, quickened the blood in her veins and muddied her thoughts in a way that was unsettling but—like her outburst a few minutes ago—exhilaratingly new.

"We could lose some really valuable things," she finished vaguely.

He nodded, instantly decisive. "No bulldozer. It's a deal. So you'd use a team to clear the cactus by hand? Machetes and whatnot?"

"I'd be here myself the whole time, to oversee the work so that nothing important was damaged. If this place was mine, I'd let the design of the restored garden evolve over a period of some days as we began to discover what lay beneath. I wouldn't plan it on paper in advance. It would be a unique, fascinating exercise."

She ran her gaze over the mazelike expanse and felt a ridiculous itch to get started at once, like a kid in a candy store. Was that the curve of a stone well housing she could glimpse between the forests of cacti? Even if the well didn't produce water, the old stone would make a dramatic accent with the right surroundings. She could see brilliant yellow flowers, too, but couldn't make out what they were. It would be *wonderful* to work on this garden.

"Tell me more, Rowena," Ben Radford invited her softly. "Make me see it. Paint it for me."

"Oh, um…" she began awkwardly, and even when she relaxed and grew more fluent, she kept waiting for him to lose interest and signal that she'd said enough.

But he never did. Instead he stayed silent. He followed the gestures she made, nodded when she emphasized a point, smiled and even laughed with her once or twice when she invited him to picture an incident from a previous project. Like the time she'd briefly mistaken a late-twentieth-century lost toy for a Civil War belt buckle because she wasn't wearing her glasses. She'd made an appointment to get contact lenses the next day.

She didn't mind telling an anecdote against herself if it made a man laugh. Ben Radford's laugh was deep and a little rusty, as if he didn't use it often enough.

"I really think that's about all I can tell you for the moment," she finished, after several minutes.

Ben nodded slowly, and made up for his disdainful failure to glance in her direction earlier by studying her with a disconcerting intensity now. What was he looking at? The too-dreamy expression in her eyes? The way her smile wobbled when she felt doubtful about something she'd said? Or was he seeing something else? Had she gone way over the top just now? What did he see? How much was he judging her?

"That's not what I envisaged when I decided to bring you in," he said.

"You expected to start with a blank canvas, so to speak, and lay the whole thing out according to a plan on paper, right off the bat."

"I guess I did."

"I could do it that way," she conceded slowly.

"But you'd rather not."

"No, because it's such a fabulous opportunity!" She clasped her hands together, then quickly separated them again. Her body language would say she was begging. "With what you've done to the house so far—that's wonderful, by the way, such a great blend of modern comfort and warmth, and authentic historical references. I'd love to do the same with this yard. To stay true to the Hispanic and pre-Hispanic heritage, while developing a space that's beautiful and usable and welcoming at the same time. You'd love it, too. I know you would."

His smile was crooked and cynical this time. "You know I would? What if I said it doesn't fit my idea of the place at all?"

She'd let her personal feelings show too clearly, and she'd assumed way too much about her prospective client. Putting on a blank, polite face, she told him, "Then we'll do whatever you decide. You're the client, Mr.—Ben. Or you would be," she corrected herself quickly, "if you decided to contract me for the project."

She didn't think that he would. Their initial dealings with each other this morning had been too awkward, and he was the kind of man who made quick, incisive decisions that he didn't rethink.

Even now, after they'd found some common ground, there

was something in the air that she couldn't put her finger on, a kind of tension that made her uncomfortable and which she wanted to escape from as soon as she could. Her therapist, Jeanette, would probably want her to identify the tension's exact origin in their next session, but Rowena wasn't convinced she should risk taking a closer look at it.

"Tell me why I'd love this idea of yours," Ben said. "How can I know? Convince me. How do *you* know? You seemed pretty sure just now."

"Because I saw what you'd done with the house," she explained simply. "That couldn't just have been the work of decorators. I could see one person's unique vision there. I assume that person was you."

"You're right. It was me. I said no to half of what the interior designer wanted, not to mention—" But he stopped.

He narrowed his eyes, looked down at the tips of his fingers and rubbed them together almost without seeing them. Was he still thinking of the picture Rowena had painted? Or was this an absentminded interest in the brilliant color of the dye that stained his skin.

"My wife thinks this whole idea is insane," he said abruptly. Then he swore under his breath and muttered, "I have to start remembering to call her my ex!"

Rowena didn't know what to say.

Ben picked up on her awkwardness. "I'm sorry. I hadn't planned to say that out loud." He gave her a sharp glance, as if wondering what on earth had made him apologize to someone like her for the second time in the space of half an hour.

"It's fine." She kept the polite facade in place.

"But you probably didn't expect to find yourself discussing my divorce," he persisted.

"No. Your bio that I found on the Internet said you were happily married," she blurted out, then mentally swore. *Oh, shoot!*

Ben Radford swore right out loud, and he didn't say anything so mild as *shoot.* "We maintained the fiction for quite a while, but I'm afraid the Internet information is out of date. If I sound bitter about it, there are reasons."

"So what went wrong?" she blurted again. Oh, this was getting worse and worse! Just because he'd let a couple of details that he clearly regretted already slip, that was no reason for her to keep this same conversational ball rolling. It was as if his forthright Irish housekeeper had slipped truth serum into their coffee. "Forget I said that," she added quickly.

"I'll answer, if you want."

"No, no please."

"Let me answer," he insisted lightly. "I need the practice."

She laughed before she could stop herself—oh Lord, what would he think now?—because it was the same thing she'd thought about him, some minutes ago, when they'd reached their first uneasy truce.

In dealing with men like Ben Radford, she definitely needed the practice.

"You have to laugh, don't you?" he said. He wasn't, though. He wasn't even smiling. "Either that or punch walls. Which hurts, I've discovered." He rubbed his knuckles to illustrate the point and made her laugh again.

Like Ben Radford himself, she wasn't all that accustomed to laughter.

Her twin, Roxanna, laughed a lot.

Rox was bright and bubbly and confident, as well as creative, disorganized and quirky. She lived in Tuscany now, having fallen hard for a wealthy Italian businessman who loved her sizzling personality. She'd been the stronger, healthier twin at birth, while Rowena had been in and out of hospitals for years as a child, with respiratory problems and a heart defect that had required more than one operation to correct.

Formed by these childhood experiences, the differences between them had persisted into adulthood. Where Rox enjoyed parties and music and crowds of interesting people, Rowena liked the meditative silence of the research libraries where she tracked down her garden history and the fresh air and beauty of the gardens themselves. Where Rox turned men's heads with her dazzling smile, Rowena became flustered and confused at male attention.

A serious clinical anxiety disorder had taken her out of the dating game completely for the past couple of years, and despite the huge progress she'd made under the guidance of her therapist, she knew she had some distance still to travel.

"I've never been divorced," she blurted out. "Or married. Or engaged. Or even very serious."

"You strike me as *very* serious."

"About a man. Was what I meant."

"I'm teasing you, Rowena." She felt foolish, until he added unsmilingly, "Because if I don't undercut your advantage a little, I am about to make myself very, very emotionally naked, telling a virtual stranger what went wrong with my marriage."

"Oh, please don't feel you have to do that!" She pressed a hand to her cheek, stricken at the fact that she seemed to have drawn out a vulnerable side to Ben Radford that she wouldn't have thought could exist.

He wasn't listening. "After I sold Radford Biotech, our divergent money styles became irreconcilable. I could phrase it that way."

"Mmm," she agreed politely.

"Do you think? How does it sound? I need more feedback than that." He looked at her, and only now did she see that those dark eyes had softened, crinkling at the corners, inviting her to take this lightly.

She still didn't fully understand the man's motivation, but okay, sure. He was the client, after all…

"Too formal," she said solemnly. She tapped the end of her pen against her bottom lip, while those eyes of his kept watching her.

"You're right." His mouth barely moved when he talked. Everything came out as a cynical, tight-lipped drawl. "How do I put it more simply?"

"You had different life goals?" she suggested. "Or, no, differ*ing* life goals."

He gave a brief, crooked grin. "That's not bad, Dr. Madison, not bad at all. You're right. *Ing. Differing*. A subtle but significant improvement. It implies polite, ongoing disagreement. And says nothing whatsoever about what really happened."

What did really happen? she wondered.

"Needs a little more, though," he went on. "A kind of one-two-punch approach. Any thoughts on that?"

"But the two of you will always remain friends. That's what you'd say if you were movie stars. And you'd still say it even if you couldn't stand being in the same city as each other at the same time."

"We would. We'd say exactly that. Heather will love it. Maybe I should write it down for her."

He was still smiling at her, in his crooked, cynical, smoky-eyed and almost dangerous way, and all at once it was too much. It seemed more like flirting than anything else, and Dr. Rowena Madison just did not *do* flirting.

She didn't know how.

And she didn't want to learn.

He was standing too close. Rowie could sense his superior height and strength and bone-deep confidence like a gravitational pull. She could detect the finer nuances in the delicious way he smelled. The tantalizing scent of expensive male grooming products floated on the clear, dry Southern California air and seemed to belong there. It gave Rowena a dangerous, illusory sense that she belonged, too.

Belonged where, exactly?

The adrenaline rush generated by her earlier boldness was ebbing fast, leaving her with a million familiar doubts.

"You can stop teasing me now, Mr. Radford," she said stiffly.

"I told you to make it Ben."

"Yes, but I'm withdrawing to a more formal level to save us both from embarrassment later on."

"You mean because of this uncomfortably personal conversation? Even though on the surface we're treating it as a joke?"

"Yes."

He heard a noise and glanced through the old gate to where he could just glimpse the driveway that curved in front of the house. A car sped around the curve and jerked to a halt.

"Unfortunately, it's going to get even more personal any second," he said. "And a lot less of a joke. This is Heather now."

Chapter Two

Heather Radford caught sight of Rowena and Ben standing by the courtyard gate just as she stepped out of the low-slung yellow sports car, so she came along the side of the old adobe toward them, instead of going to the front door.

"My lawyer's valuation of joint assets," she announced by way of a greeting, and dumped an impressively thick binder of papers into Ben Radford's hands.

Rowena felt almost comically inadequate when she considered the thin quantity of papers on her own clipboard. It was like a two-door compact car owner coming bumper to bumper with someone driving a brand-new Ferrari.

This woman had serious paperwork!

And if it wasn't an actual Ferrari she was driving, it was something with the same flair.

"I'll take a look at it later," Ben said. "Heather, this is Dr. Rowena Madison, who's doing some work on the garden."

His voice had changed since their flirty conversation a minute or two ago. It was harder, tighter, with his English origins prominent in the clipped vowels. His face had changed, too. In the space of an hour, Rowena had seen him as the arrogant, impatient businessman, the intelligent connoisseur and the charmingly cynical flirt. Now she was shocked to see him as a human being through and through, with a beating, vulnerable heart.

He *minded* about the divorce, she realized.

Minded horribly, in a whole lot of ways that went bone deep and that he hadn't even begun to come to terms with, yet.

For a moment there, she'd thought his light approach to the subject meant the opposite—that he didn't care a bit. But now she could see she'd been wrong. He made those drawling jokes about it to mask the anger and failure and pain—mask them from others and from himself. He talked about it because he was still too raw to keep it to himself. He shrouded himself in a successful businessman's arrogance because this was probably the first, and certainly the worst, failure he'd ever had to deal with in his life.

And at some level, he had no idea that this was what he was doing.

"*Dr.* Madison?" Heather echoed sharply. "You're a doctor and you have to take a second job as a gardener to make ends meet?" She was a tiny, gorgeous blonde with bright-blue eyes, flawless porcelain skin and a pert nose, and she wore a cream silk trouser suit that would have taken out Rowena's monthly dry-cleaning bill in a single hit. "Boy, did you pick the wrong specialty!"

It would have been a funny line, if the sarcasm level hadn't been so high. Rowena had the impression that Heather could be a very funny woman when she wanted to be—funny and clever and captivating and even more ruthlessly cynical than Ben.

"I'm not a medical doctor," Rowena said, her awkwardness rising back to where it had been just before she'd let fly at Ben Radford half an hour ago. "I have a Ph.D."

"Ah, now it makes sense. There's no money at all in academia. Wait a minute, though. You have a Ph.D. in actual gardening? You can do that?"

"I design and restore historic gardens, yes. My Ph.D. dissertation involved—"

Heather wasn't interested in the subject of Rowie's dissertation. She trained an accusing look on her not-quite-ex-husband. "How much work are you having done in the yard? You're bringing in someone like this. I bet you're landscaping the whole damn thing!"

"Not quite the whole damn thing, Heather. I've decided to leave the cattle runs alone," Ben drawled. "The beasts seem happy enough with grass. I'm just doing the section behind the house."

"Just? That's an acre! More! And, let me guess, we're not just talking about a few deliveries of dirt and flowers. This is going to be hugely expensive, isn't it? You're pouring yet more money into this impossible place, and it's going to mess up the valuation and slow down the divorce. You're doing it deliberately. I'm not fooled, Ben! Not for a second!"

"And *I'm* not doing it to be difficult," he said tightly. "For heaven's sake, Heather! You knew I wanted to restore the whole place when we bought it."

"When *you* bought it, against my wishes. When you sold a brilliant, high-profit company for half or even a third of what you could have gotten if you'd waited another few years, just so you could mess around with money pits like your precious gallery and your precious casting agency and your restaurant and this wretched *historic* ranch that's already soaked up a gazillion dollars. It makes zero sense! And don't tell me again that you were bored."

"I was, though," he said curtly. "Horribly bored. I'd done everything I wanted to do with Radford Biotech. I'd made plenty of money and I didn't want to hang on to it just so I could wear myself out making even more money doing more of the same thing. Heather, we've been through this a hundred times."

"Yes," she said bitterly. "And nothing changes. Which is why we're getting divorced."

"Is it?"

"Yes! So please, if you have any vestige of feeling left for the time we spent together, don't mess up my lawyer's incredibly careful and conscientious and *fair* valuation with this insane landscaping plan."

She snatched the binder back from him, turned on a heel that was way too high for such a maneuver and stalked back to the car with her shoes cracking like gunshots on the paving.

Wa-a-ay better gunshots than Rowena's own shoes had made when she'd attempted a similar exit, she noted with a twinge of self-mocking envy. It was the Ferrari versus the two-door compact, all over again.

Ben followed his not-quite-ex-wife, with that familiar, vinegary feeling flooding into his stomach.

They used to be happy, the two of them. Heather could bewitch a man, when she wanted to. Twelve years ago, as a very focused and overserious biotechnology student, he hadn't had a clue why she'd chosen to bewitch him.

"I just fell for you," she'd said later, but had added something that was possibly more honest. "I saw the potential."

Fell for him, saw the potential, then made improvements.

He'd already spent most of his adolescence building up his body as an antidote to the crippling loneliness and brutality of his expensive British boarding school, but he'd never taken any interest in clothes. Heather supervised his grooming and his wardrobe, boosted him out of his solitude and seriousness in a hundred energetic and very determined ways. And since he didn't like failure, he had recognized that everything she wanted for him was necessary and important.

On the business front, she supported him in applying for commercial patents on his ideas instead of his original plan of going into academic research, and helped him start his company while he was still completing his master's degree.

He'd respected her for all of it and had kept the respect for years. He'd loved her, and considered their marriage to be as close to ideal as marriage could get. Practical. Workable. Companionable. A success. In fact, he still didn't want to deny the years they'd been happy together. Why backdate their failure that far?

Heather was no airhead herself. She'd come to England on a college scholarship, and she had ambition as well as brains. When she'd shelved her own plan to become a research chemist in order to put her energy into helping him build Radford Biotech, he'd seen it as a sacrifice on her part.

Now he wasn't so sure. Had she viewed him as nothing more than a diamond-encrusted meal ticket all along? The prospect galled him, and made him question his own judgment.

He'd first put forward the idea of selling the company around two and a half years ago, at a time when he'd also begun to think seriously about starting a family. Heather had been against the sale from the beginning. "As far as I'm concerned, the company's still in its infancy. Its potential is barely tapped."

"Look at me, though, Heather," he'd argued from the heart, in a way he rarely did. "I'm in a business suit sixteen hours a day. My frequent-flyer miles could get me to the moon and back on a free first-class ticket. I never even get into the labs to play around with ideas anymore, let alone have a chance to do anything else that interests me. You used to tell me I was too serious when we first met, now you want to push me right back into that box. I'm not interested in that box anymore.

There are other challenges out there, other frontiers. What's it all for?"

"Oh, around five hundred million in pocket change, maybe?"

"Don't we already have more money than we can spend? I never get time to spend *any* of it. And I've never cared about cold cash for its own sake, you know that."

He'd talked about wanting to enjoy his business interests, wanting to apply his mind and his energy to something new, wanting to give a percentage of their growing fortune to carefully chosen charities, wanting to have kids who would actually know what he looked like because he would have time to spend with them occasionally, wanting to buy a house and some land that was unique and really worth something, not just a mega mansion amongst a dozen others in the billionaire version of a gated community, but Heather had hated all of those ideas.

She'd almost been frightened of them.

And she'd been adamant that she didn't want kids.

She'd come from a difficult background. An unhappy family, poverty and debt and struggle. She'd made herself into the woman she was through sheer gritty determination, brains and hard work. She wanted to keep climbing the ladder of success higher and higher, and she seemed terrified by the idea that Ben might invest in business interests that didn't pay off—that they might have a few million dollars less in the bank, five years from now, rather than a hundred million more.

She had an unrealistic, gut-level fear that they would lose everything and end up in the gutter. He began to understand that no fortune would ever be large enough for her, no financial security blanket ever thick enough.

He tried to get her to see why she was like this, that it was sourced in unresolved feelings about her childhood, and that it was a problem. He suggested therapy, but she wouldn't listen. "I'm a strong person, Ben. I know what I want and what I don't want, and I don't intend to change. Is that wrong?"

He'd kept trying, for almost two years, but their dealings with each other only became angrier and more distant, with no compromise possible on either side. When he'd sold Radford Biotech, Heather had yelled at him for three days, then didn't speak to him at all for a month. When he'd bought the Santa Margarita ranch and tried to share with her his vision of how beautiful it could be, she'd started threatening divorce.

Even then he didn't give up on his marriage. His own father had bullied his mother for years. They'd been a terrible match, after the first sizzle of desire wore thin. They'd divorced when Ben was fourteen. That was why he'd been packed off to boarding school, to keep him away from the ugliness. The fact that he'd been utterly miserable at boarding school wasn't an issue for his parents. They'd never asked if he was happy, and he'd never told them. But he'd vowed then with an icy kind of idealism that he wasn't going to repeat any of their mistakes.

He wasn't a quitter, he wasn't used to failure, and he wanted to turn this around.

But marriage required commitment from both parties, not one, and Heather wasn't interested in trying, just in getting her fair share. That valuation of assets she'd presented to him and then snatched back again just now was the product of months of bitter wrangling between them.

Heather wanted as much liquid finance as she could possibly argue for. When it was safely in her hands, she planned to invest it in a mix of reliable stocks and gilt-edged securities to make it grow and grow for the rest of her life so that, like Scarlett O'Hara in *Gone With The Wind,* she would never risk being hungry again.

Ben suspected she wouldn't even attempt to marry for love, next time around. It would purely be a business transaction—the best dollar value she could get for her assets of beauty and brains and social ambition. He was bitterly angry with her, bitterly disappointed in his own utter failure to get her to change, and deeply sorry for her at the same time. None of these emotions left much room for love, and all of them had shaken him to the core. Hell, he never intended to go through something like this ever again!

"Explain something, Heather. Why does my plan to landscape Santa Margarita affect the valuation?" he asked as she climbed into her car.

"Because you're going to pour a huge amount of money into it, and that kind of thing never recoups itself in the value of the house. You'll put in a quarter of a million dollars, and the valuer's estimate on the house will go up by twenty thousand."

"Even if that's true, does it really matter?"

"Oh, you mean, what's a stray couple of hundred thousand dollars between friends?"

"Yes. That's exactly what I mean."

"I want what's mine, Ben."

"Aren't you getting enough already?" Many millions, as he well knew.

"Are you suggesting I didn't contribute as much as you did to the success of Radford Biotech?"

"Heather—"

"Forget it." She put up a hand, then turned the key in the ignition, and said above the flare of engine noise, "Our lawyers can talk about this. We're sure as heck not going to get anywhere with it on our own."

"No, we're not," he agreed. It was one of the few things left in their lives that they did agree on.

"Someday, Ben, your charmed life will come to an end."

"That's not a threat, I hope." Threat or not, it chilled him to think that she wished him ill.

"Of course it's not. I just hope that when it happens you have the right insurance, that's all."

"I think our definitions of the word *insurance* are probably very different."

"Very! Don't give me your spiel on the subject. People and memories and priorities and values. I've heard it before. And by the way, I think you're making a huge mistake with whatshername." She thumbed over her shoulder in the general direction of Rowena Madison and the derelict garden.

"You mean the project or this particular consultant?"

"Both." Heather snapped her car into gear, revved the engine again, then spun around with a spray of gravel and dirt that showered desert dust onto his trouser legs and shoes.

"Thank heaven we never had children," he muttered as he watched her drive away. It was the only piece of positive thinking he could drag from the whole mess.

Then he turned to find Rowena Madison standing quietly nearby, awaiting his attention. She must have come out here through the side gate when she'd heard Heather's car starting. Her serious, enormous eyes were fixed on him with a troubled expression in their dark-blue depths. Her willowy figure had an angular look. Tightly bent elbows, hunched-up shoulders. The set of her limbs created a force field of distance.

She had a very nice body, he decided, although she didn't seem to be aware of the fact and certainly had no idea how to dress herself to her own advantage. He assessed her impatiently for a moment.

The severe colors and tailored silhouette were totally wrong, especially with her hair—apart from one wandering strand—folded up so tightly on the top of her head. Her eyes would be incredibly beautiful if she did anything whatsoever to help people notice them. Someone should damn well tell her that she didn't have to imitate a nineteenth-century schoolteacher in order to look like a competent professional.

The escaped strand of bouncy dark hair blew across her face and snagged against her full mouth. She let it stray between her nicely shaped lips and began to chew on it, and he had a ridiculous impulse to pull the strand away and scold her.

Chewing on your hair, Dr. Madison? An appalling habit. Don't ever let me see you do it again! And do something about the way you dress!

Suddenly she reminded Ben of how he'd been himself, fifteen years ago, at around eighteen or nineteen—so much going for him in some areas and so clueless in others. If he could change, then so could she.

Heather couldn't. She didn't even want to try…

But he wasn't thinking about his ex-wife right now.

He wanted to grab Rowena Madison and stand her in front of a mirror and tell her, "Look at yourself! Attractive, intelligent, perceptive. Don't be so afraid to let it show. Don't be afraid to take risks and to feel. Make an effort. Change. Fight. And please, don't be afraid to let other people get close to you."

Although not me, he mentally revised, because I'm not ready to get close to anyone.

Just when he really was about to scold her about the hair chewing, she caught herself at it, frowned in disgust, hooked the strand out of her mouth and tucked it back behind her ear.

"Much better," he murmured.

"Oh…" She was clearly upset that he'd seen.

"I was about to tell you to stop."

"Um, thanks. I try not to do it. I've almost stopped. But sometimes it happens when I'm thinking about something else."

Right now, Ben realized, the *something* else would be his divorce, and that line he'd let slip about not having kids. She'd almost certainly heard him.

Damn.

"But at least I don't bite my nails anymore." She held them up for his approval and threw him a wobbly yet triumphant smile.

He gave her what she wanted. "Good. That's great." It was like congratulating a five-year-old who'd eaten her green vegetables three nights in a row, but he meant it, too. "Bad habits are pretty hard to let go of sometimes," he told her.

"Mmm, so how long were you married?" she asked.

"Eleven years."

"I guess it would be hard to let go, after such a long time."

"I meant your nails. You let go of biting your nails."

"Oh, gosh, I'm sorry." She looked stricken again. "I didn't mean to say that your marriage was a bad habit."

"Hmm. Maybe it was."

"Well, you'd be the one to know…"

They'd been so clumsy with each other this morning. Angry. Not listening properly. Saying too much. Laughing when they shouldn't have. Getting it all wrong. In Ben's experience this didn't usually happen with strangers. You were usually too careful and polite to generate that level of complexity and emotion in a conversation when you hadn't met someone before.

"It's fine," he told her shortly. "I don't like mess, and I don't like failure. A divorce means both, whether it happens after eleven months or eleven years or half a lifetime."

She nodded. "And you're right, it would be so much harder with kids."

"I'm sorry you heard that."

"I won't call the tabloids about it." She gave a sudden, captivating grin that changed her whole face. She looked mischievous and perceptive and alive. "You can safely stick to the script, Mr. Radford."

"You mean that Heather and I will always remain friends?"

"That's the one."

They smiled at each other again, but the softer moment didn't last.

Ben didn't understand, in hindsight, why he'd felt compelled to spill so much to a woman like this—a stranger and someone who surely had problems of her own—about his impending divorce. And he suspected suddenly that she hadn't been at all taken in by the cynical tone with which he'd tried to mask his sense of bitter failure.

Already, after less than two hours spent in his company, Dr. Rowena Madison knew way too much about him.

Chapter Three

Four weeks after submitting her draft garden plan and costing to Ben Radford, Rowena concluded that he must either have abandoned the project or given the contract to someone else. He hadn't struck her as the kind of man to sit on a decision for a long time, nor one who would vacillate back and forth. Maybe he'd concluded that his ex-wife was right and that the whole idea was a huge mistake.

Oh, yes, she'd heard that part, too, although she didn't think Ben knew that.

She wasn't surprised that he hadn't chosen her. There had been too much awkwardness between them for one short and supposedly professional morning, too many moments of hit-and-miss understanding. He would choose a landscape designer who hadn't experienced those instant and unsettling windows into his soul as he talked about his impending divorce—someone much safer, in other words.

Rowie knew she'd never forget his final muttered words as Heather Radford had driven away.

Thank heaven we never had children.

Beneath the arrogant, successful facade suggested by his business suit, he was a complex man. Strong yet with a vulnerable streak that he didn't like admitting to. Good-looking yet by no means skin-deep. Passionate and creative and alive in a way that hadn't so far made him very happy, she guessed.

For some reason, he fascinated her and frightened her at the same time. He was very definitely not safe.

Which made it all the more fortunate that she would probably never see him again.

And yet that wasn't how she felt about it, as time went by. She didn't want total safety anymore in her life; she wanted some danger.

"What are we going to work on this spring?" Jeanette asked at their next therapy session at her office in Santa Barbara.

"Men," Rowena told her firmly.

Earghh, why had she said that? She should have disguised it in therapy-speak, at least!

Not that Jeanette was very into that kind of jargon. "You're dating someone?" she asked, sounding interested and ready to approve.

"N-no. But I think I'm ready. I'm sure I am. Only, I don't know if the kind of man I'd like to get involved with would see that I'm ready."

Jeanette laughed. She was a practical woman in her late forties, interested in present-day problem-solving, not endless examinations of childhood influences, traumas and dreams. She expected Rowena to come to their sessions with clear-cut goals they could work on achieving together, and the approach had been wonderfully successful so far.

Rowena had first started seeing her a year ago, after

moving to California from Florida and contacting her on the recommendation of Francine, the therapist she'd been seeing back east. The first goal Rowena had expressed to Francine two years ago had been, "Being able to leave my apartment on my own."

Yes, really. Whether you labeled it agoraphobia or anxiety or just plain wimping out, Rowena had gone through a horrible, paralyzing period when she hadn't been able to leave the safety of her own or her parents' apartment without someone she loved and trusted by her side coaxing her through it.

She'd made a lot of progress since then, including the move across the country.

Her parents had been concerned about the move initially. California? All on her own? What if the panic attacks came back?

But Rowena had known it was the right thing. Her twin sister, Roxanna, was living in Italy with her gorgeous husband, Gino. And Rowena was only in Florida in the first place because she'd fled to her parents in their retirement condo after her anxiety problem had become too severe to handle on her own.

It was time to strike out, to find her independence, her courage, her self-sufficiency and her place in the world. Apart from her parents, she'd had no ties in the Fort Lauderdale area, and no important ones in New Jersey, where she and Rox had grown up. As well, the opportunities for the kind of garden design that interested her were few and far between on Florida's low-lying, sandy terrain.

A couple of major garden design contracts in the Santa Barbara area sealed the deal, and after a year in her new, light-filled apartment, with an office in a building full of dentists and lawyers and architects nearby, she loved it here and felt at home. There was an enormous range of climates and plant life along the Pacific coast, as well as so much fascinating history.

Jeanette was great, too. The therapy sessions worked. Whether it was finding the right person or just a readiness for change in Rowena herself, they worked. She had gone from "Being able to leave my parents' apartment" to "Being able to speak at professional conferences" and now she felt ready for "Being able to date."

"Although, to be honest, I think this one's going to take a while," she said.

"You're stronger than you know, Rowena," Jeanette said.

"Sometimes I might agree with that statement!" She sighed. "But sometimes it seems as if I take three steps forward and two steps back."

"We all do that. Three forward and two back is still progress. Just don't underestimate those forward steps. Write them down."

"And the backward steps, too?"

"Let's just focus on the forward ones. Let the backward steps go. Dwelling on those doesn't help."

Spring unfolded.

Then summer.

And then—

"This is Ben Radford," said a male voice on the phone on a Monday morning in September. "Are you still interested in working on the garden at my Santa Margarita Ranch, Dr. Madison?"

Ben Radford. Good-looking, wealthy, cynical, forbidding Ben, who'd made Rowena brave enough, in the space of one morning, to want some danger in her life.

Rowena sat heavily into her swivel chair, the brimming mug of coffee she'd just made for herself splashing a small puddle onto the desk in front of her. "I sent you the draft plan and costing for the project six months ago," she said blankly.

There was a short, impatient silence down the phone, then, "I take it that's a no."

"Um, n-not exactly a no."

"Then what?" More impatience. "Your estimate has doubled?"

"Not that, either. More of a let me consider."

"If you're fully booked with other projects, I can wait. Just give me an exact timetable." His deep, liquid English voice seemed ridiculously familiar, even though they hadn't spoken in so long. *Thank heaven we never had children.* The line had echoed in her head for weeks afterward. How often had she heard a man express that degree of emotion in his voice?

She'd been listening to other men's voices lately, but they hadn't made her forget Ben Radford's. She'd been on several dates, and although they hadn't led to long-term relationships, they'd been a success in her own terms.

She hadn't panicked, canceled or run. She'd been able to eat and talk and ask questions. She hadn't felt her own emotions and reactions like the throb of a sore, swollen thumb, the way she used to. She'd relaxed and enjoyed herself. She'd kissed two men, smiled and said good-night to them without feeling that she had to make some stammering, apologetic explanation about not going to bed on the first date and…

Yes.

Progress. Forward steps, which she'd measured and made note of, as Jeanette had suggested, while letting the backward steps go. It was great.

And it all seemed to evaporate in an instant at the sound of Ben Radford's voice, bringing back all too familiar sensations of breathlessness and agitation that she hadn't experienced in a long time.

"I'm booked, but there are some windows," she said. "It's just…" She trailed off, then found the professionalism that always helped her through. "Most people don't take six months to make up their mind on whether a design proposal is acceptable, Ben. What's going on?"

"I decided it was best to get my divorce and property settlement finalized first," he said. "It took longer than I expected."

"Oh. Of course. I'm sorry." Sorry that she'd pushed for his reasons.

"But things are a lot better now."

For me, too, she almost said.

Although maybe that wasn't true, because a familiar impulse to cut and run, which she thought she'd dealt with, suddenly surged again inside her. It was all she could do not to gabble without pause for breath while starting to sweat. *I'm sorry, I've just looked at my schedule, I am fully booked for the next fifty-three years, you'd better find somebody else, goodbye.*

Don't do it, Rowie. Didn't you want the danger?

"Let me look at my calendar," she said instead, after a deep breath. Still more flustered than she wanted to be, she dived at random into the ledger-size planner on her desk and found her time heavily booked for the week after next, and the following two weeks after that.

"First, can I ask how you plan to proceed?" he said, before she could turn the pages of her planner again.

Despite the many and varied garden proposals she'd put together since seeing Santa Margarita, Rowena found that her memory of Ben Radford's place was detailed and acute.

"We'd need to work in at least two phases, and probably three," she said. "First, I'll have to see what we're working with. An exploratory phase, clearing out the jungle that's there now. Then I'd be able to return here to put together a detailed plan, which is likely to be split between a hardscaping phase—putting in any new structures—and then a planting phase. Costing's included in all of it, of course."

"And the exploratory phase could take place when?"

She flipped her planner again, backward this time, to

confirm what she'd been ninety percent certain of all along. Apart from two site visits, which she could easily reschedule, the pages in her planner were blank between the day after tomorrow and the end of next week.

He'd been right to wait, Ben concluded two days later, when he saw Rowena Madison cross the tarmac at San Diego Airport's small commuter terminal down near the water.

If he'd tried to proceed with the garden project while dealing with the messy details of his divorce and property settlement, he would have ended up hating every flower and every paving stone, and probably thoroughly disliking Dr. Madison herself— if she'd managed to last on the job. He would very likely have sent her packing with his negative moods, his distance and his distracted mental state before the project was even half-finished.

And if he'd gone with a larger local landscaping company, he would never have experienced this astonishing kid-in-a-candy-store feeling welling up inside him now.

He realized that he was itching to get started on this thing, and began to understand how much it had to do with the painful failure of his divorce. He wanted the validation of something new, something fabulous, something that worked.

He'd cleared his schedule as much as he could for the next nine days. Just a few business meetings and conference calls, as well as a couple of evening commitments. Dr. Madison might envisage him supervising her ideas from a safe distance with the occasional stroll around the perimeter of the dirty work, but he had a very different plan in mind. He was going to shed his heavy business suits like a snake shedding its skin. He'd put on jeans, T-shirts and work boots, and get his hands dirty right along beside her.

She saw him as she came through the door and into the terminal building, and she smiled. Carefully professional and a little wary, he saw. She had a gorgeous mouth but the smile was wobbly, and her deep-blue eyes were shadowed by her tension-tightened lids.

Well, he couldn't blame her for the wariness, if her memories of their morning together six months ago were as fresh as his were.

They'd rattled each other that day.

They'd gotten right under each other's skin.

They'd told each other far too much.

Now they shook hands. The sober gray cuffs of her jacket were too long. They hid her wrists completely, but couldn't hide the way she'd had to work at her hands to get rid of the garden stains. Manicured in clear polish and softly moisturized, they nonetheless had a slight roughness to the palms that told him she had every intention of getting dirty, too.

"Thank you for meeting me in person, Ben," she said, visibly struggling with the informality of his first name. "You really didn't have to. In fact I expected—" She frowned.

"You thought I'd send a car for you?"

"No, I assumed I'd drive a rental. When I return for the next two phases I'll bring my own car, but this time it was in the shop for some work. I've made a rental reservation. We arranged that I'd come out to Santa Margarita for a meeting at three, didn't we?"

"We'll cancel the car rental reservation. And as for our meeting, that's still on, but meeting you at the airport beforehand seemed like a better idea, since I was in the city already."

"About the car," she persisted stubbornly, setting that mouth in a straight line. "I will need my own transportation."

"You can drive my SUV if you need to. That would be easier for you, in any case, with equipment and samples and so forth, wouldn't it?"

"It would be, yes," she agreed carefully.

Her caution seemed habitual. Ben compared it with her sharply accurate and quite passionate outburst about his self-importance six months ago and was intrigued.

What would she be like when the polite and bland veneer slipped? It *was* a veneer, he felt convinced, and in fact it had already slipped a couple of times, when they'd talked about his divorce. She had brains, heart, humor and perception. He wondered why, too often, those things just didn't show.

"Any bags to wait for?" he asked.

"Um, a couple. As it happens." She winced slightly, and a few minutes later he understood why.

Three large matching suitcases.

Gray, of course.

Ben wanted to tell her that black, gray and navy weren't the only colors a professional woman could be seen with in public while still keeping her reputation intact. Some high-flying female executives were daring enough to try cream or burgundy, or even florals. Some of them showed a bit of skin. Instead, heaving her baggage from the carousel, he exclaimed, "What on earth do you have in these? Sample paving stones?"

"Research material."

"Books?"

"Mainly."

"They feel like encyclopedias."

"Well, most of them are about that big, I guess. For some reason, publishers don't put out small reference books." The smile was almost flirty for a moment, but then Ben could actually, visibly, see her pulling back, like a scared cat skittering across a slippery floor. The smile turned into a frown, like the sun disappearing behind a cloud. The body language tightened. She stepped farther away.

"We'll get a cart," he said, while fighting an out-of-left-field curiosity to know which of her conflicting personality traits she expressed in what she wore when she was alone.

There must be *some* occasions when she let her vibrant side free. What did she wear to bed, for example? Flannel pajamas? High-necked cotton nightgown? Strappy satin slip? Or maybe—a long shot, here—she wore nothing at all....

"Will I be able to keep some of them at Santa Margarita?" she asked.

Nope. Had to be the cotton nightgown. With full-length sleeves.

"Some of them?" he echoed, having to force his concentration. "Where will you keep the rest?"

"At my motel."

Oh, hell, they should have worked all this out in advance!

"I thought you'd prefer to stay at the ranch," he told her. "There's a separate guest wing, and I've had my housekeeper prepare it for you. We won't be in each other's pockets."

"No," she agreed awkwardly. "I mean, it's a big house."

"It's up to you, of course, but I thought you'd be more comfortable staying on-site, with meals on hand and no driving back and forth. The nearest motel I'd recommend is some miles away from Santa Margarita."

"That's...that's very kind of you. Thank you."

"You can come and go as you want, of course," he reassured her again. "There's a separate entrance. Your private life is your own."

She still seemed uneasy about it, however, and her ongoing discomfort got under his skin. Why did the damn woman have this effect on him?

Rowena adjusted her thinking.

She ditched the idea of lining the trunk of a zippy little rental compact with a layer of heavy-duty plastic so she could ferry plant or paving samples from garden centers back to Santa Margarita. Ditched the anonymous safety of a budget-priced room at a blandly elegant chain motel. Ditched the prospect of several hours in which to gather her breath and her cool before heading out to Ben Radford's land-grant ranch at the respectable and prearranged hour of three o'clock this afternoon.

She'd be driving his SUV, staying in his guest wing and, before she got to any of that, it seemed that they were having lunch. He announced the fact in an offhand way as he maneuvered out of the airport parking lot in his midnight-blue European car. Rowena hadn't taken in the make or model; she was too busy sinking into the luxury of its butter-soft leather seating.

And then he hit her with the lunch thing.

"At La Jolla," he explained. "Not quite on the way, but almost. There's a great seafood place that overlooks the ocean. It's on the market, and I think it might be an interesting addition to the Radford Lateral Enterprises portfolio so I'm scoping it out. We can celebrate the start of the project with some champagne."

She wanted to ask him if a long, expensive lunch was really necessary, but when she rehearsed the words in her head they sounded prim and disapproving and, really, did she need to be that way? She should remember why she was here.

To work on a really fascinating, historic, possibility-laden Spanish-land-grant ranch's mission-style garden.

Ben Radford's garden.

"Great," she said firmly. "And while we eat, we can talk about some ideas."

Five minutes before reaching the restaurant, they passed the corporate headquarters of Radford Biotech. The low white building was set in a manicured sea of green turf, mown in a crisscross pattern that made it look like a plaid blanket spread on the ground.

The reflective glass of the windows shone in the sun. The massed plantings of exotic grasses and desert shrubs had a majestic, almost architectural quality, and the asphalt driveway that led into the parking lot was as fresh and smooth as the frosting on a wedding cake.

"That's my original outfit," was Ben's four-word commentary, and Rowena didn't like to crane her neck to take a backward glance at the building because he seemed so offhanded about it.

And after all, the corporation was no longer his.

It said something about him, though—about his eye for detail and beauty in the building and its surrounds, and the hard work he must have put in to create something so successful.

She didn't totally buy the offhandedness, either. "You sold it all? You didn't keep a partial share?"

"I sold it all," he said, then added almost ruefully, "And then three months ago a big parcel of shares came back onto the market and I bought them for twenty percent more per share than I'd gotten for them last year. Just as my ex-wife predicted, the value's still going up. So I do have a stake in the old place again, now—around ten percent."

"You didn't want to let go."

"Wanted a way to keep reading the stockholder reports, make sure the new management structure isn't driving the place into bankruptcy."

Rowena remained politely silent for a moment.

Ben added on a drawl, "Okay, I admit it, it was pure sentiment. Didn't seem as if it should still bear the Radford name if I wasn't a part of it."

"But you didn't want a controlling interest or any active involvement?"

He laughed. "With Radford Lateral Enterprises I haven't got time!"

Inside the restaurant, they were given a table by the windows with a glorious view of the ocean. Rowena took off her suit jacket and let the air-conditioning cool her bare arms below her sleeveless silk top, while she watched the waves.

Watched them, wondering why she couldn't think of anything to say to the man seated opposite, until she heard him murmur, "No two ever come in exactly the same."

"Oh, the waves? Yes, I've been watching them for way too—"

"I noticed. I always do it, too." He closed his menu.

"Do you?"

"So don't stop. We'll both watch them."

"All right."

They smiled at each other, and looked at the ocean meeting the sand until the waiter came back to take their order and Rowena realized she hadn't even looked at her menu yet. She quickly chose a seafood pasta with salad on the side, and Ben asked for grilled mahimahi with mango salsa. He ordered champagne, too, although he only allowed himself a small half glass.

For Rowena, a half glass was enough to slow the meal down, make it go a little fuzzy at the edges. Or was that the hypnotic effect of the water rolling and crashing onto the beach? She forgot to talk about the garden. At least, she forgot to talk about Ben's garden. He asked her about other major projects she'd done, and she found herself telling him in too much detail about roses in Italy, fountains in Oregon and orchards in Maine.

This wasn't the kind of place where they hurried you through so they could slap down fresh sets of silverware and seat the next clients. The two of them could have stayed here all afternoon. It was after two by the time they left, and she walked beside Ben to his car, feeling as if she'd been wrapped in a cocoon of well-being and expectancy.

"I'm looking forward to this, Ben," she said, on an impulse, forgetting to find him intimidating. "It's like a treasure hunt. I'm sure we'll find some fascinating and valuable things in that jungle of a yard."

"Valuable?" They approached his car, and it gave a little whoop as he unlocked it.

He looked as if he might go to the passenger side to open the door for her, but she beat him to it with a couple of determined strides. She didn't want him standing there just inches from her while she climbed inside. He went around to the driver's side instead, without breaking that easy stride of his.

He paused at this point, leaned his forearm on the warm roof of the car and looked at her across the dark-blue expanse, sure of himself as always. "Is that important? That what we find should be valuable?"

She looked back at him, passenger door open, one shoe tip resting on the metal rim beside the seat. "Oh, no, no, I'm not talking sell-it-on-eBay valuable. It's less tangible than that."

"Yeah?"

"I...I can't really explain."

"Try," he invited her, and she realized how much he'd gotten her to talk over their meal, rather than talking himself.

He was still doing it. Not over a meal, this time. Over a car roof.

He rested his chin on his arm and watched her, his eyes hidden by sunglasses, while she struggled to find the words. "You know in movies, it's always about gold, isn't it?" she said.

Gold... The sun glinting on his hair, reflecting off the sunglasses, darkening the golden tan on his arms and face. He was way too good-looking, even when he frowned.

"Chests of jewels and coins," she went on, fighting the way he distracted her. "Things that anyone and everyone can see are a treasure, at first glance. But sometimes there's value in a piece of paper or a chunk of gray rock or a handful of pottery shards, and not everyone sees that. So many people are blind to it."

"Some things have value purely because you choose to see them that way, you mean. Sometimes you have to look below the surface."

"That's right." She couldn't tell if he was really interested. "That's part of it."

The car roof was pleasantly hot, after the chilly and powerful restaurant air-conditioning. She stroked the gleaming blue metal without thinking too much about the action, just enjoying the warmth, suit jacket still hanging over her free arm.

"Or because they tell a story, maybe." He was still looking at her, his expression impossible to read.

"That, too," she said. "I love those kinds of stories. The questions you can't always answer. The mysteries you can sometimes solve. Who made this? Who broke it? Why is it here?"

"Stories that you yourself can read and understand a little better because of your specialized knowledge, where someone else might toss the item in a garbage pile and never know."

"Yes."

"Which only makes the treasure worth more to you, because its value is your own private secret. Like a little girl seeing fairies when no one else can."

She looked at him in sudden amazement. So few people understood this at all, let alone managed to explain it better than she'd ever explained it herself. "How come you get that?" she blurted out. "Nobody seems to, when I say it, not even my twin sister. But then, I'm not that fluent sometimes. You know, I'm an intelligent woman, I have a Ph.D., so you'd think, wouldn't you? But no. When I'm nervous, or—"

"Like now?" he said, unexpectedly gentle, because she'd begun to gabble. She could hear it herself. "Why are you nervous now?"

"I wasn't a minute ago. But you're making me self-conscious."

"Not that difficult to do, from what I can work out." He

gave a cynical grin. "I've been trying very hard to get you to relax all through lunch."

"Oh."

"And you do, for a while, when you talk about the things that really interest you. And then something sets you off again, and we're back to square one."

"Me. I set myself off. It's not your fault." She slumped one shoulder against the curve of the car roof, disappointed in herself, embarrassed because Ben Radford saw through to the flawed heart of her so easily. Saw through to the awkward, self-doubting, thirty-one-years-old-and-never-been-kissed heart of her being.

She *had* been kissed.

Of course she had.

She'd been taken to bed, too, a couple of times, but…but…

It had been wrong. Both of those men had been wrong. The wrong guy, the wrong feelings, the wrong time and place in her life. She wondered what it would take for her to get all those things right, and couldn't see it happening right now.

"Get in the car, Dr. Madison," Ben told her softly, seeing too much, as usual. "You're getting car roof dust on your arm."

Chapter Four

"No, I'm going to love it." Dr. Madison's eyes shone. Her gaze darted about, taking in the detail of the newly refurbished guest wing. "You kept the original door. That old wood is so wonderful. I love the colors you've chosen."

Ben hadn't gone for his decorator's initial suggestion of classic Southwestern earth tones, and the two of them had done some polite-yet-steely negotiation—"You're the client, Mr. Radford"—and ended up choosing a mix of white and turquoise and gold.

"I love the coolness and silence," Rowena finished.

"Because if you truly would prefer a motel…" he said, deliberately leaving the sentence hanging, just to see what she would say.

He could already tell that she wouldn't prefer a motel, and without wanting to be, he was intrigued by the way her instinctive appreciation for beauty and history changed her face. Her eyes widened. Their deep, beautiful blue went even darker. Her mouth softened. Her lips parted.

She forgot the nervous tension and shyness that seemed to wrap around her like a cloak too often, tightening the angles in her limbs and stripping away their natural grace. The tension and shyness made him angry with her at times. There was no reason for her lack of confidence, and he had a low tolerance for people who let their own flaws hold them back.

Well, her flaws weren't holding her back right now.

She wasn't quite smiling, but the expression was better than a smile. *Radiant* he would have called her, if he wasn't the cynical survivor of a recent divorce, who didn't go anywhere near any word that had the slightest association with brides.

She gave a gasp of pleasure at the sight of the nineteenth-century mission-oak hall seat in the entranceway, trailing her fingertips lightly across its waxy patina on her way toward the bedroom. "Oh, this is gorgeous! And this!"

She looked at the painting on the wall—a splash of vibrant colors in a landscape by a modern Italian artist who didn't really belong here, if you were going to be strict about it, but somehow the painting had seemed to fit. Ben refused to be a purist about such things.

On an impulse that he didn't examine too closely, he said to Rowena, "Come to the exhibition opening at my gallery tomorrow night, if you like art." She hesitated, and he added quickly, "I'm serious. You'd enjoy it."

"But I'm here to work."

"Not in the evenings. Anyway, your profession is so much about visual appreciation. You should go to galleries. You should gorge your senses whenever you can." She looked alarmed at his prescription, but he ignored her, impatient with her again. "And don't tell me you'll be too tired. It'll be easy. Just a hop in the helicopter, there and back."

"Helicopter…"

"Yes. I charter them out here quite a lot. I don't always feel like driving into town."

"Oh. Nice not to have to deal with the traffic." She was looking as if out of her depth again.

"So it's a deal? Dinner afterward, if we're hungry. You'll need to be ready by five-thirty."

"I…I… Okay." She spread her hands and gave a helpless kind of laugh, as if she couldn't believe he'd really been serious.

Ben wondered about the spontaneous invitation, too. What had he saddled himself with for tomorrow's event? Serial awkwardness, or a really nice night? He had no idea.

The two of them put her bags down on the handwoven rug, and she paused for a moment to assess the queen-size bed, the adjoining bathroom and the other furnishings.

"Thank you," she said. "I mean, for the suite. It'll be perfect."

"Your sitting room needs something, though," Ben said. "My decorator tried a rolltop desk in there and it looked terrible, but you do need some more surface area to lay out your work. You can use my secretary's office when she's not around." He had some loose arrangements with his staff these days, and people came and went between here and his large office suite in San Diego on an ad hoc basis. "And my conference room when you have something to show me, but I imagine you'll be wanting to work in here quite often."

"What about that old workbench outside?"

"That old thing?"

"Old is good."

"You think it's old enough to be interesting?"

"I think it's a lot older and more interesting than it looks. Truly!" Arguing her case, Rowena's hands moved expressively in the air, her hesitation about the gallery opening already forgotten. "It's so solid."

Her palms flattened over the imaginary surface and smoothed it down. It was an amazingly tactile gesture, considering the workbench wasn't really there.

"I couldn't see a single nail, let alone a staple," she said. "It's been put together using proper joinery techniques." She hooked her fingers together, in imitation of old-fashioned dovetail joints. "It's covered in 1970s paint splashes and hammer marks, sure, which gives a bad impression, but the workmanship says it's been around a good hundred years longer than that."

"I didn't realize you were an antiques expert, too. You can tell the age of the paint by the colors?"

She went shy, suddenly. It seemed to happen the moment the conversation turned personal, Ben realized. "Oh, I'm not an expert. Really. Not at all."

Those expressive hands had turned jerky and were now bunching into tight little fists. She brought a thumb to within two inches of her mouth before she remembered that she'd given up biting her nails—and how come Ben himself remembered the conversation they'd had about her bad habit when it had taken place more than six months ago.

"But you pick stuff up," she went on, giving a clumsy shrug. "Colors date like anything else. Mission brown and harvest gold are a seventies cliché. I mean, I have picked up a little knowledge, working with old gardens. It's a hobby, nothing more. An appreciation." She'd gone into gabble mode.

To calm her down, he asked, "So what would have to be done to it before you'd want to bring it inside?"

"Strip it back, smooth it down, refinish it. Something soft and subtle to bring out the grain." For one final moment, talking about the plan, she sounded sure of herself again, and he wanted to yell at her, *Stay that way, for heaven's sake!*

"I'll get Pablo and Wayne onto it tomorrow," he told her instead. "They should have it done in a couple of days."

"Pablo and Wayne?"

"You don't think you're getting your hands dirty all on your own, do you?"

He got her to smile, but it was wobbly and uncertain and forced. Was he laughing at her or with her? she clearly wondered.

Don't, he wanted to tell her. *Just be who you are, Rowena Madison, or you're going to drive me crazy very fast.*

He wasn't going to get her real self back, though, he could tell. Not right now.

Somehow the knowledge didn't stop him from trying.

She stood there while he showed her the bar fridge and coffeemaker and told her, "If you want to eat breakfast in here, Kate can bring you all the supplies. Just make a list for her and leave it on the mission seat." Rowena had only met his fifty-four-year-old redheaded Irish housekeeper six months ago, in passing. Ben wasn't convinced she was quite ready for the full encounter yet. "For that matter, she can bring you the rest of your meals on a tray from the main kitchen, but it would be easier for her if you'll eat in the dining room with me."

"Oh, of course. She…?"

"Cooks, keeps house, wrangles window cleaners and maids and repairmen. I'm keeping the two of you apart until I think she can handle you."

"Handle me?"

"She's a little shy and unsure of herself. You're pretty full-on."

Rowena flushed.

All right, she was shy and unsure of herself, Ben saw, but she wasn't stupid. She'd understood at once that he was teasing her—that Kate was the one who was too full-on. He felt as if his humor had missed the mark. Cut the ground from under her feet instead of giving her support. He was angry with himself…and with Rowena, too.

She didn't have to have these doubts about herself! She was a bright, attractive woman, locked inside the limitations of a gawky young girl.

Talk about antiques, Dr. Madison. Talk about gardens or paintings or hundred-year-old workbenches or whatever the hell you want. Just get that radiant, appreciative, *beautiful* look back on your face because that's how you should look and be all the time....

No, he definitely wasn't getting it back now. She stood there, her body language practically screaming at him. *Go now, please. Leave me alone to unpack and make this my space.*

Okay, he could do that.

"Take as long as you want," he told her.

"And then can I start?" she blurted out.

"Start?"

"On the garden. As soon as I've unpacked. I'm itching to," she confessed, and flushed again. "It would be great to get in a couple of hours right away."

"Well, sure." His turn to be awkward. He wasn't used to it, but her sudden eagerness made him feel as if he was looking in a mirror.

He always had that same hunger to dive into a new project, like a kid hopping up and down in front of the ticket window at Disney World. He felt that it sat ill with his position of wealth, success and authority, so he tried not to let it show.

In fact, there were a lot of things inside him that he tried not to let show....

"I'll make sure Pablo and Wayne are on hand as soon as you're ready," he went on, "and I'll get them to lay out some tools and equipment right away."

"Um, thanks. Only if it's convenient."

"It's fine." He could see that she really, really wanted it to be convenient.

Leaving her, he had to fight to hide the grin of appreciative recognition that wanted to spill onto his face. Maybe all
the manifold differences between them only ran skin-deep.

Ben Radford thought she was really weird, Rowena
decided. It was all too obvious.

Their initial argument and subsequent odd connection six
months ago, their conversation over lunch and beside his car,
all of that was irrelevant, now. They'd hit the real-life, nitty-
gritty start to their professional relationship and Ben thought
she was completely and utterly weird for talking about 1970s
paint colors and for wanting to get out and get dirty within
half an hour of her arrival.

For a few moments Rowie reconsidered.

Maybe she'd unpack like a French maid, folding everything exquisitely in tissue paper, ironing her underwear,
laying her vintage 1930s silk and lace nightdress and robe
beneath her pillow. Maybe she'd take a nap or a bath or lie
down on that inviting expanse of bed wearing nothing but a
towel, cucumber slices and a cleansing facial mask. Maybe
she'd sip herbal tea and read her horoscope for the next year.

Or not.

She'd begun to yawn at the very thought, and she didn't
have tissue paper, cucumber slices or a horoscope book with
her, anyhow.

Most important, did it really matter if she didn't fit with
Ben Radford's idea of suitable womanhood?

Heck, no!

Instead she slid the suitcases full of books under the bed
and dumped her clothing in drawers, apart from the nightdress
and robe, and a couple of outfits that she made the token effort
of hanging in a closet. She made a quick list of breakfast
supplies for Kate—orange juice, coffee, milk, whole-grain
cereal, fresh fruit. Impatience sang in her blood, and it took

her roughly ninety seconds to discard her gray suit in favor of jeans, a lilac T-shirt, a red baseball cap and good, clunky work boots.

She wanted to be in the garden.

When she got there, she discovered a wheelbarrow, a thick pair of brand-new leather gardening gloves, a row of tools with metal heads and wooden handles and several types of cutting implements ranging from lightweight pruning shears to a bow saw with a heavy serrated blade, all of it lined up at the edge of the shaded courtyard veranda for her inspection.

Yum. She loved gardening tools.

She slid her hands into the gloves and stepped off the veranda into the jungle of cacti. Winding her way through, peering beneath tangles of greenery and piles of discarded junk, it took her twenty minutes to reach the far side, where a low, crumbly stone wall marked the formal end of the garden.

Climbing onto the wall, she could look out to the fenced pastures where sturdy Santa Gertrudis cattle grazed, or toward the already-restored stables where Ben had installed four horses for trail riding over the property, or back in the other direction to the house with its rows of semicylindrical terracotta roof tiles baking in the fall sunshine.

Half closing her eyes, she began to plan.

If this place were mine, what would I want?

The images came quickly.

Water splashing somewhere. Colorful tiles. Shady places to sit. Traditional motifs and details. Native plants. Plants brought by Spanish missionaries. The smell of orange blossom and herbs. Flowers in colors so bright it would hurt to look at them. Trees hanging with fruit. The textures of stone and wood. Old things. Living things…

The afternoon sun heated through the baseball cap and felt like a hand pressing warmth onto her hair. She sat down on the rough wall, not caring about dirt on her jeans or the insufficient padding on her butt. She closed her eyes fully and began to feel drowsy. The plans became more like dreams.

Old-man cactus with gnarled limbs reaching into the blue sky. Golden fish in a pond. A child's pull-along toy with sturdy wooden wheels. The thwack of a baseball on a wooden bat in the field beyond the wall. Kids laughing...

Hey!

Her eyes flashed open again and the drowsiness fled. You couldn't incorporate laughing kids and thwacking baseballs into a garden design. Things like that were beyond her control, and didn't seem likely to form a part of cynical, difficult Ben Radford's life anytime in the foreseeable future.

Even though they belong.

To Santa Margarita, if not to Ben himself. There was such a welcoming warmth about the place. It *wanted* kids...a whole loving, sprawling family...even if Ben didn't.

It's not your business, Rowena.

She was thirsty and hot. Scrambling off the wall, she skirted the edge of the cactus jungle and reached the house in just a couple of minutes in search of cold water. She found Pablo and Wayne instead, waiting for her on the veranda, beside the garden tools.

They greeted her, and there was an awkward moment in which she had to decide whether it should be Rowena or Dr. Madison. And because she still had that ill-fitting impression of kids' laughter and baseball sounds in her head, she messed it up, just said, "Uh, yeah, hi," and realized she didn't know which of the two men was which.

They looked very similar—two stocky men with dark coloring and work-hardened hands, one in his early thirties and one around ten years older—but they spoke completely differently. One had a broad Texan drawl, while the other barely knew a word of English and communicated with gestures and smiles and lacings of another language.

This would be Pablo, she decided.

Mexican Pablo, Texan Wayne.

Easy.

She asked Wayne for water, then directed the men to start cutting down the tangles of cacti in the shadow of the house and forgot about the phantom sound of laughing children, and Ben Radford's complicated personality, and the gallery opening she'd promised to attend with him tomorrow night— forgot about anything but the work at hand and the refreshment of frequent gulps of cold water for the next two hours.

Chapter Five

"Pablo, here. This. Lift."

With an air of great confidence, energy and enthusiasm, Rowena was happily calling the two men by the wrong names. Standing unseen in the shade of the veranda, leaning against the whitewashed adobe wall, Ben watched her doing it, wickedly reluctant to intervene. He usually found it very irritating when people made that kind of mistake, but there was something about Rowena...

The woman was cute, you had to admit.

He knew he was seeing her at her best, like this. The stompy boots that she wore with such an odd degree of grace. The streaks of dust on her cheek. The clashing colors of purple T-shirt and scarlet baseball cap. The mix of authority and childlike excitement in the way she spoke.

"Yes! I knew it, guys! This is the old well, under all this. That's fantastic, look at the beautiful old stone. Can you see that? Great, Pablo, yes. Lift that right off and we can get a better look."

She darted in to show him, then moved nimbly out of the way. She had the baseball cap pulled low on her forehead to shield her eyes from the sun, and somehow it emphasized the strong line of her high cheekbone.

Ben wondered how in the heck she'd gotten to the age of thirtysomething and still clearly didn't know that she was beautiful.

"Wayne, we'll need to organize something better than a wheelbarrow for carting all of this away. We're going to be suffocating under it. Maybe I should ask Ben—" Saying his name, she looked toward the house, saw him and stopped. "Oh. Hi." She pressed her hands together.

How long have you been watching us? her face and hands said. And why are you scaring me by doing such a thing? Her movements already threatened to lose their litheness and enthusiasm, giving her joints the familiar angularity that made Ben so impatient.

She wasn't cute sometimes!

He came forward, wanting to conjure up some power to coax her to relax. She was like a young Thoroughbred mare who galloped brilliantly in an open, grassy field and froze up as soon as she reached the racetrack. The contradiction drove you crazy, but what could you do about it?

Some horses, and some women, were hard to settle and school.

"You say this is the well?" Maybe if he could get her attention away from herself and back to what interested her much more... He really did not want to have to deal with such a complicated and very female personality for the next eight or nine days.

"Yes, see that lovely curve of stone?" she answered. "Feel it." She modeled the action herself, taking off the soiled leather glove and running her hand along the roughness of the newly exposed section, taking care to avoid the protruding spines from a pad of prickly pear.

Ben reached out and did the same thing. The stone was warm. Its texture tickled and scratched his palm, and the dusty residue felt oddly pleasant on his skin. He knew he would never have thought to appreciate the sensation if she hadn't called his attention to it. He had a sudden flash of a mental glimpse of her hands running over softer things. Silky fabric, lathered soap, male skin…

The flash came and went too soon. It left him with too many questions and a very powerful need to pull back. He didn't want to be attracted to her. He just didn't need that kind of challenge. And Rowena was totally the wrong kind of woman for a quick, meaningless affair.

"I don't know if it'll still have water in it," she was saying. "It might need to be dug out, and you'll want to get the water tested for purity. What is it that the EPA tests for now? Something like a hundred and twenty-nine different chemicals? If we're lucky, we may even find a date, or something, carved into one of the stones. And an original bucket. That would be fantastic, too."

"You look as if you're having fun." The word tasted odd in his mouth. All of his new and growing enterprises, grouped under the rather whimsical corporate name of Radford Lateral Enterprises, were supposed to be fun, but he was finding it hard to shake off the superadult cloak that Heather had been so insistent he wear. In a perverse, unwanted way, the cloak had grown comfortable and too familiar, a protection against the possibility of failure.

"Oh, we're having a great time!" She gave a little frown and a self-conscious laugh. "At least, I am. Don't know about Pablo—" she smiled at Wayne "—and Wayne here." She gestured at Pablo.

Both men looked down at their boots and then up at their hat brims, not knowing how to tell her about her mistake.

"Wayne and Pablo," Ben corrected her gently, since the guys themselves obviously weren't about to do so.

"I'm sorry?"

"You have them back to front." He rested a hand on the immigrant's shoulder. "This is Wayne." Pointed at the Texan. "That's Pablo."

"Oh." She laughed and flushed. "Oh. Right."

"Pablo's family is third-generation Texan. Right, Pablo?"

"Fourth on my mother's side, second on my dad's. I average it."

"As for Wayne here, he's from Romania, married to a lovely California girl he met while she was working in Bucharest as an interpreter with an American corporation. They've only been back in the U.S. for two months."

"Taking class at night," Wayne supplied. "Improve English."

"His dad was a big fan of American Westerns. Right, Wayne? His brother's name is Clint."

"Sorry," Rowena said, still blushing but kind of grinning at herself, too. "My Romanian isn't all that fluent." Then she took a big breath, turned her mouth down and said, "So much for the ethnic stereotyping of names. Guys, is this the moment when I can ask you to stop calling me Dr. Madison and make it Rowena instead? You've been doing it all afternoon, and it makes me feel...you know...prim, like I should be wearing bifocals and a twin sweater set. Rowena, okay?" she repeated, for Wayne's benefit.

"Ro-wayna," he echoed, giving it a lilt and rhyming it with his own name.

"Thanks, that's great." She was still bubbly over the discovery of the well, and as far as Ben was concerned, she could stay excited about it for the rest of the day, if it stripped her of her shyness, put that sparkle in her voice, made her forget to be embarrassed about switching peoples' names and making too many assumptions.

Made *him* forget a few things, too.

"Pablo, tomorrow morning, can you hitch up the tractor and trailer?" he said. "Rowena's right. We're going to have a mountain of dead cacti soon. You're not taking it all out, though, Rowena, are you?"

"This close to the house, I am," she answered. "We need to let in the air and light and space, leave room for some lush greenery and running water that you'll be able to see from inside, and some gorgeous Spanish tile. Farther from the house, the garden should be less formal, and there should be more plant species that are local to the area. And I thought a working kitchen garden would be great, an authentic reference to what would have been here long ago."

"Not very pretty, though."

"Oh, no, there you're wrong!"

"Yeah?" Not many people told Ben Radford that he was wrong these days. It was strange that Rowena felt able to do so, when she was so uptight about so many other things.

"If a kitchen garden is laid out right," she was saying, "it can be every bit as beautiful and pleasing as shrubs and flowers."

She'd returned to work as she spoke, using the protective gloves to clear rattling bits of dead cacti from around the well. Its shape began to emerge more completely, but not fast enough for Ben.

"Borrow those gloves?" he asked Wayne, who held them flapping in his hands. The man was smiling at Rowena, appreciative of her energy, not thinking to put the gloves back on his own hands to help her.

So Ben did it, instead.

Yeah, he could get into this, he decided. The sun on his back, the satisfaction of moving his muscles, of seeing his achievement unfold immediately as the pile of dead cacti grew. Fun. After a couple of minutes he rolled up the sleeves of his business shirt and wished he'd replaced it with something simpler, to go with the jeans he was wearing now. At least he wasn't sporting a striped silk tie.

Rowena gave him the occasional sideways glance, as if she didn't quite believe he was capable of being such a hands-on type. She was waiting for the novelty to wear thin, and she was right. He didn't really have time for this today.

"I have a message from Kate," he told her.

"Oh, yes?"

"She wants to know what fruit you like and says I have to get you to stop working and take a shower now because she's not feeding you a four-course meal if you're dirty." Something made him add, "Even though I happen to think you're terrific when you're dirty."

Pablo gave a snort of appreciative laughter, and Ben realized too late how easily the comment could be heard two ways. Actually, Pablo had probably read it just the one way, and it wasn't the way Ben had intended. Damn. If she got hold of totally the wrong impression, it would be a bloody nuisance.

"Um, well, I'm definitely that," Rowena said, looking down at her dust-mottled T-shirt and jeans and carefully choosing a face-value interpretation. "But is it nearly dinnertime already?"

"It's almost six."

"Hmm. Explains the shadows. Where do we put the tools overnight?"

"You don't put them anywhere. These guys do. You take that shower."

He couldn't help watching her all the way along the veranda to the guest wing, thinking about the shifting moods and impressions he'd had of her all day. Was it really only this morning that he'd picked her up from the San Diego commuter terminal with those heavy suitcases? He was about to sit down with her over four of Kate's gourmet dinner courses, and right now four courses didn't sound like long enough.

Four courses took way too long to eat, even when one of them was only a delicate green salad. The way Kate kept creeping in and out to serve the courses and remove the empty dishes didn't help. She would mouth out things like, "Cracked pepper," every now and then, exaggeratedly signaling that she didn't want to be a nuisance, in a way that was far more intrusive than actual speech.

"I hate when she does this," Ben muttered.

"Does…?"

"Creeps. Mouths things. She only does it when she thinks I'm dating. When it's business, she bustles in and out, quite cheerful and normal."

"Well then, you're right. She definitely shouldn't creep. Because this isn't a date." Rowena certainly hadn't dressed for one. About the only thing she could claim for the outfit, after this afternoon's dusty T-shirt and jeans, was that the pastel skirt and top were pressed and clean.

Ben hadn't been out in the garden long enough to get dirty, but he'd changed out of that incongruous business shirt and into a cotton sweater that hugged his strong frame too well. Rowena remembered how his arms had looked when he'd rolled up the shirtsleeves, the tanned muscles working easily and the contrast of skin and fabric reflecting the contrasts she'd begun to discover in the man himself.

So forbidding, sometimes, and…and…bad-tempered, really, like a brooding lord in a dark and crumbling English castle. Yet at other times so down-to-earth and funny. Cynical yet enthusiastic. Impossibly wealthy yet happy to be hands-on. None of it fit. All of it stirred something new and danger-ous inside her.

She wanted to know him better, but where could that possibly lead?

"Kate, stop!" Ben ordered out loud.

The Irishwoman turned in the doorway, balancing her piled tray. "What is it now, then, Mr. Radford?"

"Come and meet Rowena properly. You're making her nervous."

So Rowena met Kate and learned in the space of three bewildering, and strongly Irish-accented, minutes that she'd come to the U.S. as a widow on vacation at the age of forty-three when her only son turned twenty-five and got married. She'd had a whirlwind romance with a Las Vegas croupier, "who didn't look nearly as good in the daylight, I'm telling you, darlin'!"

Not surprisingly, the marriage hadn't lasted. "My divorce party was brilliant!" But Kate had stayed and worked in the kitchen of a huge Las Vegas hotel for seven years before retiring to the quieter life of being Ben's kitchen queen and housekeeper here at Santa Margarita. She had brown eyes with sooty lashes, fair Irish skin, wrinkles that told you she smiled a lot and hair whose vibrant burgundy red was un-ashamedly not natural.

Ben managed to communicate to Rowena that Kate terror-ized him in myriad ways, and that if she had any sense, she'd be terrorized, too. Rowena decided inwardly that she *didn't* have any sense, because she already liked Kate a lot.

After the potted biography, Kate stopped creeping, but then the meal crept, instead. They had to wait at the table for the berry soufflés, and there just wasn't enough for them to say by this point in the evening.

Rowena was tired after rising early to make her flight, and there was a limit to how much even she could talk about old wells and dead cacti. The more she tried to be interesting, the more her wits deserted her. It was a familiar pattern, and she could tell Ben was bored.

"I'm sorry. You're bored," he said, just as she hid a yawn behind her hand. "And tired. This is a date meal she's given us, too. I don't normally get four courses, with a gap between each one."

"Two would have been plenty," Rowena agreed, privately deciding to take the offer of a tray in her room whenever she could.

"Would you like dessert and a pot of hot tea on a tray in your room?"

"Oh, that would be great!"

Then they both said, at exactly the same time, "I'm sure you have things to do."

It was funny, but not funny enough to make either of them change their minds about where to finish their meal. They'd finish it right now.

Rowena retreated from the dining room, happy to be alone. Ten minutes later, when a knock sounded at the big wooden door of her guest suite, she was already wearing her vintage silk nightdress and robe, splashed with lace and pink roses.

Which turned out to be somewhat inappropriate when she discovered Ben himself standing there with the dessert tray in his hands, instead of Kate as she'd expected.

"*That's* what you wear to bed?" he blurted out, as if he'd been wondering about it.

"Um, yes."

"Why don't you wear that kind of thing for business appointments?"

"My *nightgown?*"

"I mean the colors, the lush— I can't talk about clothes. And I'm making you self-conscious."

"I should have thought that it might be you, not Kate, and stayed dressed." She ran her hands awkwardly down the fabric, and he took a sharp breath and looked away.

Then they apologized to each other multiple times, until he put a stop to it by saying in a tone of unbrookable authority, "Look, it's a perfectly respectable robe." She heard his impatience. "I think we're okay."

"Yes. Yes, we are."

She wasn't, of course. She crossed her arms over her front but then remembered that she needed to take the tray. Holding her hands out for it, she felt the time-worn silk fabric brush over her nipples, the friction chilly yet sensuous. A man like Ben probably saw perfect-bodied women in string bikinis lounging around elaborate pools on a regular basis, so it was idiotic to think that an ankle-length nightdress and robe remotely qualified as a provocative ensemble.

So why hadn't he given her the tray?

Why was he just standing there, looking as awkward as she felt? Why had his gaze dropped to her mouth, where she could feel it almost like a caress? What was that strange sensation in the air? It was like the sing of wind through wire. The moment you tried to listen to it, it went away.

"Don't tell Kate that the soufflé went flat," he said. "Shall I put the tray on the mission seat?"

"Yes, please."

He did, and she stood back and watched him. Smelled the clean, male scent that came from his clothes and his skin. Wanted him, suddenly, with a rush of confused heat that seemed to come out of nowhere.

What on earth was she doing? What was she thinking? To let her senses come alive to a man like this while living under his roof, a man she was working for and who scared her silly half the time.

She'd let the same thing happen once before, in Italy, and it had brought on a crippling anxiety attack that had lasted for days. It was the beginning of the horrible period when she hadn't been able to leave her parents' apartment without either Mom or Dad beside her. She hadn't been able to finish the Tuscan garden project—or not directly, anyway. She'd had to send her sister to put in several weeks of damage control.

And what was Ben thinking?

Because it was coming from him, too. She wasn't totally naive. She could tell when a man lingered a little too long in a woman's company, when he looked too closely, when his eyes got that blurry, steamy quality.

"Wh-what will Kate do if we tell her about the soufflé?" Rowena stammered. She didn't want Ben Radford to look at her that way. He was light-years out of her league and they both knew it.

"She'll say *I told you so,* because she did tell me."

His eyes went crinkly around the outer corners when he gave a smile that wasn't cynical. His face had a seasoned look to it sometimes, the look of a seasoned, experienced man—someone who'd worked hard and seen a lot, way more than she had.

It jolted her to glimpse these depths in him, and stirred something deep inside her. The woman who earned Ben Radford's trust and commitment, after the burn and bitter disillusionment of his divorce, would need some impressive qualities if she was to match him in the ways that counted. Rowena suspected he would be very slow to conclude that he'd found the right one.

If such a woman even existed.

If he ever let himself even try.

"It's a form of domestic cruelty to carry soufflés out in the cold air, apparently," he went on lightly. "We're criminally callous. We were supposed to stay in the dining room."

"For the sake of the soufflé?"

"These sacrifices have to be made. Surely you see that."

She laughed. "It'll taste just as good flat."

"Don't tell her that, either, I'm warning you."

"I won't." She had to laugh again, and he was smiling, too—a broad, unselfconscious grin that defied any woman to look away from his dark, good-looking face, or refrain from smiling back. Right now Rowena felt as if she could go on smiling at Ben Radford forever.

"She'll think you have no taste in food and start serving you canned spaghetti, with applesauce for dessert," he said.

Such a smile!

And me in my robe…

"Um, thanks, Ben. Good night."

"Hope you sleep well, Dr. Madison." His gaze dropped to her mouth again. Contemplating a kiss. Painting her mouth with it in his imagination. Wondering how she would feel and taste, and how she would respond. Hungry for the sensation because, with his divorce, it was something he hadn't let himself experience for a while.

She knew it…

He stepped closer, reducing the distance between them to a few shimmering, electric inches. She could feel his heat. His hands began to lift from his sides, ready to touch her where all those luxurious roses splashed across her body. She took a sharp inward breath and felt the cool movement of air across her lower lip, because she'd already parted her lips in expectation.

He was very sophisticated.

He'd done this before.

Maybe he *had* done it since his divorce, a lot, with all sorts of willing women…and she knew the moment when he decided not to do it. He added softly, "Dream about the garden."

"I…I'll try."

She didn't draw a decent breath until she heard his footsteps fading along the adobe brick outside.

Thinking back on the day as she ate the sweet, fluffy soufflé, with its rich berry syrup and sides of vanilla ice cream and hot tea, Rowena honestly didn't know which of the many fine and ludicrous moments to groan about more.

Ben's reaction to the weight of her suitcases. Her mix-up over Wayne's and Pablo's names. The phantom sounds of baseball and kids laughing, as she sat with her eyes closed in the garden, dreaming of how it would one day look.

The day could have been much, much worse, though.

Ben Radford could have followed through on that electric moment just now and kissed her.

True, it would have been worse if he'd kissed her, Ben realized as soon as he'd reached the solitude of his own room.

What he could possibly do about the damned woman, he didn't have a clue. He'd stood there at the door of her suite with that wretched soufflé on a tray for several minutes longer than he'd needed to, *flirting* with her.

Flirting with her deep-blue eyes and her pretty bow of a mouth, flirting with that astonishingly sexy rose-covered drape of silk and lace that clothed her body and rustled and flowed whenever she moved.

And she was the wrong kind of woman to flirt with. An acne-plagued seventeen-year-old computer geek could have told him that.

After a bad divorce—and was there any other kind?—a man needed to get back in the game, but he needed to do it right.

Divorce made you cynical. It stripped your trust down to the raw. You needed to play for a while, as the healing slowly took place, if it ever could. In his own case, he had doubts on that point.

You needed to flirt with and date women who understood the game, women who didn't get serious too soon, women who didn't ache over every notch of male attention on their pretty belt.

Rowena Madison was absolutely and unquestionably not that kind of woman.

She seemed innocent enough to be burned by a mere kiss, to feel it down to the depths of her soul. If she went any further, Ben suspected she would be shocked and shattered into a thousand pieces by the power of her own sensuality and would need a man to lavish her with the most—

Hell, what was happening to him now? He paced his room, willing his sudden and all-too-physical arousal to go away. The very thought of igniting that kind of flame in Rowena, of lavishing her body with magic, had made his own body leap to attention, ready to act.

The word was *curiosity* but it sounded too tame and thin. He felt way more than curious about the potential in her response. Images played in his mind like video clips. Her hand touching the stone wall that curved around the old well. The neat yet sensual way she ate. The way she looked at colors and inhaled scents. What she chose to wear when she tucked herself into her bed all on her own.

He couldn't do it, though.

He couldn't follow through on this. She was too vulnerable, and they were too wrong for each other. He had so little to give, when she deserved and needed so much. He'd failed so badly with his divorce. He never intended to fail that way again.

Forget it, Ben.

Just forget it.

Right now.

Deliberately he nixed his plan to read a book in bed before turning out the light and went along to his office instead. He had reports to read, budgets to go over. He welcomed the shift of focus and the chance to get his feet back on hard, cold, businesslike, ruthlessly successful ground.

Chapter Six

The air began to vibrate.

Hot and dirty in Ben Radford's dusty mess of a garden at four o'clock on Thursday afternoon, Rowena couldn't identify the sound at first and didn't realize that it had anything to do with her. Then as it grew louder, she recognized it was a helicopter—a private, chartered helicopter. Shadowing the sun for a moment, it passed overhead, ready for landing here at Ben's ranch, on his own personal helipad.

He used them regularly, he'd told her—hopped between the ranch and San Diego or the ranch and Los Angeles at least twice a week. Probably climbed aboard beneath that whirring propeller without a moment's thought, still stuffing papers into a briefcase or talking on the phone, whereas she…

Her chest went tight.

That's right. She would be flying in one of these intimidating contraptions herself. Tonight.

Ben had asked only yesterday if she wanted to go with him to the exhibition opening at his gallery in San Diego tonight, and she'd said yes because at the time it seemed much easier than saying no. In any case, he'd virtually ordered her to go. At the time, too, he hadn't made such a thorough and unsettling assault on her awareness. She'd seen no reason to say no.

Just over twenty-four hours later, the whole idea seemed a lot scarier, and the almost threatening beat in the air as the helicopter landed and slowed its rotor blades didn't help. Rowena had never been in a helicopter before, and her stomach was not too politely asking her if it could stay at home. People like her, if they went to gallery openings at all, certainly didn't go to them via a private flight.

The prospect challenged her plans about what to wear, what to say, how to react to Ben, how to manage to eat, and she wondered how she could possibly fit during such a glamorous evening, especially by his side. The impending reality of the event shattered her sense of peace and contentment and cast a shadow over the rest of the day.

Until now it had been great.

Ben had spent the whole morning and another two hours after lunch working side by side with Rowena, Pablo and Wayne. He was strong and hardworking and cheerful, she'd discovered, and he didn't mind getting dirty. The smears of dust looked unfairly good on his body, too, emphasizing a masculinity that wasn't nearly as civilized as his business suits suggested.

They'd cleared a mountain of cacti, discovered a pattern of drainage channels made of time-scoured reddish brick and what looked like a household dump. On the surface, it was just a heap of broken pottery and rusted tools, but Rowena sent Pablo out to the hardware store in search of garden-strength sieves so they could go through it properly and not risk missing anything.

Pablo was skeptical. They were going to sieve through all that danged dirt? Why?

"Haven't you ever wanted to hunt for treasure, Pablo?" Ben asked with a slow grin, reminding Rowena of the odd fact that he seemed to understand her prickling sense of eagerness and curiosity about things like this.

He'd looked at her for a moment as he asked the question. His habitual terseness had gone, and they'd smiled at each other as if sharing a secret. Her heart had lifted helplessly. She'd felt so much at ease with him today, barely remembering how intimidating he could be or how hopeless she herself could be.

At just before four, however, he'd taken his perfectly engineered Swiss watch out of the breast pocket of his discarded cotton sweater, muttered, "Gotta get going," and had disappeared inside without a backward glance.

In the ten minutes since, Rowena had begun to feel all too thoroughly the way her tired muscles ached, and the grit that irritated her eyes. Her two workmates were complaining about the afternoon heat. Maybe Pablo was right, and it was pointless to tackle the garden so carefully and slowly, just on the off chance of finding treasure. Maybe she should order in a bulldozer, after all. Her spirits began to slide.

Now the chopper was here, panicking her with its implications and its demands.

"Don't embarrass a major client," the slowing rotor blades said. "Don't embarrass, don't embarrass, don't embarrass." The blades stopped.

Wasn't it early? Ben had said she should be ready to leave at five-thirty. The possibility that she'd misunderstood the arrangement added to Rowena's sudden jitters. What if he couldn't wait and went without her?

The almost physical slug of disappointment that hit her in her gut told her how much she was looking forward to the evening, despite all her doubts. It scared her, too. She couldn't let herself fall for a man like Ben.

Kate came out with cool drinks and a plate of cut-up fruit a few minutes later and provided an explanation for the chopper's early arrival. "Mr. Radford has a meeting, so he flew one of his accountants in. He told me you should stop work whenever you need to, Rowena, in order to be ready in time to leave at five-thirty for the opening."

"So h-he still wants me to go?"

Forthright Kate threw her an assessing glance. "You don't have to be so nervous about it, darlin'." Her Irish accent was pretty and lilting. "They're not so bad, the chopper things. You get a lovely view. But I wouldn't go on an empty stomach, like. They can swoop around a fair bit."

"Thanks for the tip. I'll have some fruit." Rowena forced several pieces down past the nervous lump in her throat, gave Pablo and Wayne some final instructions for the day and headed inside.

Only to be faced with the woefully inadequate contents of her wardrobe.

There was really just one possibility—the Italian designer cocktail dress that her twin sister had sent across the Atlantic for their shared birthday.

The great thing about having an identical twin was that you knew each other's gifts of clothing would fit, and now that she was living in Italy, Roxanna took full advantage of the fact. The downside of having an identical twin with Rox's confidence and flair was that when she sent a designer dress, she sent a designer dress like this one.

It was black and glittery and barely there in all the wrong places. Rowena had never worn it—she'd never had the right perfect opportunity and hadn't been brave enough to wear it on any lesser occasion.

Like, say, to the grocery store, just for the heck of it.

Maybe this should be her next goal to work on with Jeanette. "Being able to wear the clothes my sister sends me."

She'd already told Jeanette that she would dress up more and go for bolder or more dramatic styles and colors if she could summon the courage to throw away her emotional safety net in public. The only place she'd managed to do so was in bed, in private, with her extensive collection of gorgeous vintage nightwear.

But then she had a stubborn moment and decided, why wait for Jeanette's input, since she already knew what Jeanette would say? Why not go for it tonight, all on her own?

Because a secret, hidden part of Rowena's soul loved the dress. Loved its promise. Loved the richness of the beautiful fabric, the fine workmanship showing in every detail of its finish, and the gorgeous sound of the silk lining rustling against the outer skirt.

She'd only packed it to come to Santa Margarita at the last minute, after a phone call from her mom in Florida. "Make sure you take something dressy, just in case. He's a wealthy man. Dad looked him up on the Internet."

"So did I."

"If he has a cocktail party, or something—he's bound to have things like that—you'd hate to be caught in office wear when every other woman was wearing a beautiful gown."

True.

Rowena laid the dress on the bed and looked at it, daunted by how much it would show off her body and yet admitting to herself that she was thankful for the way fate had backed her into a corner.

If Rox knew about tonight, she'd be cheering her twin on. *Enjoy it, Rowie. Embrace your sensual side.*

Pushing her jitters out of the way, Rowena decided that tonight was definitely the right time for a forward step.

She took a shower, washed her hair, wrapped herself in a

towel and managed a halfway-decent blow-dry and some makeup. Then she put on the sexy black lace Italian designer underwear that Rox had sent her the birthday before last, and the sexy spike-heeled Italian designer shoes Rox had sent for Christmas, and climbed into the dress.

Oh, shoot.

That's not really me, in the mirror.

Rowena turned away from the unsettling sight before it panicked her into doing something stupid like putting on a clean pair of jeans and a cotton top instead. She made a brief and doomed attempt to do something about the revealing neckline, then heard the chopper blades starting up again outside. *Don't embarrass, don't embarrass, don't embarrass…*

For better or for worse, it was showtime.

Wow.

Ben had the sense not to say it out loud. Rowena already looked like a sleek, pedigreed black-and-white pet rabbit discovering too late that she was on a blind date in the middle of a trackless forest with the Big, Bad Wolf. *Wow* would only make her worse.

She also looked fantastic.

Or she would, if she could just damn well relax.

The dress clung to her body like a second skin, the fabric light and shimmery. The inky black contrasted with her skin and brought out the dark sapphire of her eyes. In killer heels, with hair that bounced and shone and swung every time she moved, Rowena Madison was as tall and every bit as attractive as a model, if only she knew it.

She had a little more padding than you ever saw on the catwalk, however—enough to give her a curve or two, and to make the pale slopes of her breasts above that delectably cut neckline wobble just the right amount when she walked.

Or sort of hobbled, really.

Clearly, she wasn't accustomed to the shoes.

Instinctively Ben took her arm as soon as she reached him, and she looked grateful and nervous about it at the same time. In fact, she almost flinched—the rabbit again, wondering if the wolf was going to take his first illicit bite out of the naked wrist he'd now managed to get hold of.

She was infuriating! He wasn't that scary!

To reassure her, not sure why he noticed or cared about her nerves, Ben stroked the inside of the wrist with the ball of his thumb and they both were far too aware of the movement. She looked down at the place where he'd touched her. Her cheeks went pink, and she wobbled again on her heels.

"Steady, there," he murmured. "One foot in front of the other. Point your toes and pretend you're on a tightrope. I'm pretty sure that's how it's done."

"You do it, then, if you're such an expert," she answered, the show of spirit coming lightning fast.

He laughed. "I guess you're more at home in trainers."

"And I really, really don't think a helicopter is the place to learn in heels like these. I already feel as if I'm too far off the ground."

"It's fine. You look great. The pilot's waiting for us. And we're dropping Steve back into town, as well. Want to sit in front or back?"

"Uh…"

"How about the front? You'll get a better view." *And so will I…*

Way too much of a view, it turned out.

Rowena looked horribly nervous as she took her seat, and Ben wasn't sure if it was a fear of heights or a fear of the whole evening. Probably both. She gripped the first solid helicopter bits she could reach, and her grip was white-knuckled and unrelenting. She wasn't planning to let go of this baby until it was back on good hard ground, and they hadn't even taken off yet.

The engine noise inhibited conversation. All Ben could do was sit behind the pilot, next to his taciturn-as-always tax accountant, Steve, and keep an eye on Rowena's state of mind, as revealed by those death-grip hands and that fine-boned, tightly clenched jaw. They rose into the air, and he saw her press her lips together.

Okay, how bad was this going to be? Was she about to have a full-blown panic attack or something even worse?

But then as the pilot circled over Santa Margarita and headed for the city, something changed. Ben had seen this transformation in her before, but he was a long way from being tired of it yet. Her attention was caught by the beauty of the unfolding landscape. She forgot to be nervous and her whole body language changed.

The dark, gleaming hair swung back and forth as she turned her head, craning to see everything. She leaned forward, forgetting the unaccustomed low neckline that was making her uncomfortable, and he had to look away from the angled view of her breasts. Her shoulders relaxed, and he saw how smooth they were. Her face lit up and her lips parted, making him wonder what those lips would do when they were kissed sweet and deep and hard by the right man.

He sat back and watched, trying not to smile in sheer appreciation, inwardly lecturing himself about the fact that Rowena Madison was the last woman in the world he should let himself flirt with tonight or should even think about kissing. He was pretty certain, however, that not flirting with her would be an ongoing battle.

The chopper landed at Montgomery Field. The pilot helped Rowena out and ushered her away from the still-spinning rotor blades. She looked exhilarated and a little dizzy from the ride. Ben discovered that he was looking forward to putting a steadying hold on her arm again, feeling the soft press of her arm against his, smelling the light, sweet scent that hovered around her.

Steve climbed out, said something serious and very boring to Ben about investment property, then hurried off to grab a cab. As soon as Ben himself was on the ground, the chopper pilot returned to his controls and lifted the aircraft off the ground again, sliding it at an angle through the air en route to his next pickup point.

"So," Ben asked Rowena, sliding his arm through hers. She swayed against him for a moment, and her cheek almost hit his shoulder. He loosened his hold, alarmed by the instant response in his groin. "Not too scary?"

"Terrifying!" She grinned, her face lit up like a Christmas tree, pretty and wholesome and dazzling. "But I loved it, too. So much to see!" She took her arm again and clapped her neat hands together a couple of times like a child, as if she couldn't wait for what was coming next.

It was a long time since Ben had met a woman this innocent in her pleasure. There was a strange part of him, deep inside, that felt wistful about it, like a child with his face pressed against the window of a toy store his parents couldn't afford. Would he ever rediscover the innocence and the faith that had been ground into the dust by the bitterness of his failed marriage?

"There should be a car here for us any minute," he told her, then saw it approach across the windswept ground and cruise to a halt at the curb beyond the fenced perimeter of the heliport.

Chapter Seven

The art gallery was crowded. It was a modern, mission-style building near Balboa Park, with a fountain splashing in a front courtyard amidst lush green landscaping and golden exterior lighting. Inside, there were white walls and track lighting and large spaces where tonight's art was on show, as well as a crush of people, with more arriving every minute.

"It's amazing what you've done to this place, Ben!" several people said.

"It was so tacky before you bought it."

"Well, I wouldn't say tacky."

"It was! Trinkets masquerading as art."

"I wouldn't have dreamed of coming here."

"But you've given it the typical Radford magic touch."

"Thanks, guys," Ben replied.

Rowena soon forgot to be self-conscious about her dress, even though she'd been horribly aware of its unfamiliar cling and cut, all the way here in the rented car with Ben. For a start, many of the women here wore outfits that were a lot more glittery and revealing. And then there was her fascination with the whole event—much more interesting than obsessing over her own state of mind.

Instinctively she clung to Ben's side, accepting the occasional reassurance of his touch, using a glass of champagne as a prop, while the noise level rose and the drinks flowed.

"You're not actually drinking that champagne, are you?" he murmured in her ear after nearly an hour.

The formal part of the event was already over. Ben himself had made a short speech of welcome, before handing over to a visiting expert who'd introduced the artist and his work in glowing terms. Now Ben was back at her side, moving smoothly through the crowd or letting people come to him, which most of them did. He drew them like a magnet, partly because of his name but more because of the aura he gave off.

"It's more useful that way," she answered him, about the champagne. "Stops waiters from trying to refill it every six minutes, which would probably have scary results in my case."

He laughed, with the unwilling note that so often sounded in his voice when he did so, then waved to someone over the heads of the crowd, and they didn't talk to each other anymore for a while, which was fine. He was the subtle kind of schmoozer, she observed. He didn't make it obvious whom he enjoyed talking with and whom he was itching to escape from.

At one point he allowed himself to be monopolized by a tedious couple whose relentless talking about themselves made it quickly clear he had nothing to gain, business wise, from giving them his time and attention. You never would have guessed the fact from his manner. Authoritative handshake. Nods and smiles in all the right places.

He could put on a good pretense when he wanted to.

But who was the real man who lay beneath? The incurable cynic? No, she knew there was more.

"You've been raised well," she commented, when the couple finally moved on.

"While those two need a couple of tips on cocktail hour etiquette, is that what you mean?"

"I wasn't going to say it up front."

He turned to her. "How about you?" She saw the challenge in his dark eyes at once. "How well were you raised? Are you going to tell me up front what you think of these pieces, or are you going to politely lie?" He gestured at the shiny metallic forms filling the gallery on their black pedestals, his eyes sparking out a lazy challenge.

"How do you know I don't like them?" she blurted out, then bit her lip as she realized he'd tricked her into a confession. He seemed to be far too good at that.

He shrugged. "Just a guess. So I'm right?"

Pointless to lie politely now. "I find them too cold. And they don't…oh…speak to me."

"No, I didn't think they would." He confessed surprisingly, "They don't speak much to me, either."

"And yet your gallery chose this artist as a client."

"He's very well regarded, commands big prices—"

"Yes, I saw a few people going pale when they looked at the catalog."

"—and he has gallery representation in New York and Rome. I wanted to turn this gallery around and really make it a place for opportunities. If I don't take on some big names, I'm not doing any favors to the lesser-known artists whose work I really like. I want the rising tide to float the little boats as well as the—" He stopped.

"The big ones," she finished for him, helpfully, since he seemed to have forgotten the words.

He wasn't listening. "There's Heather," he muttered, looking over Rowena's shoulder toward the far side of the gallery. "What the hell is she doing here?"

He watched his ex-wife in silence. Rowena didn't swivel her head in the direction of his sharp gaze, but kept her focus on Ben himself. In the space of seconds he'd turned wary and tightly wound. Where was the man she could often talk to with such surprising ease?

Gone.

Completely hidden behind the cool, arrogant facade.

Distant, the way he'd been the day he and Rowena had first met.

"Aah," he said after a moment, still on a mutter, still watching with covert intent. "So that's the motivation. Now, should I steer clear, or get it over with and go up to her?"

"I...I don't know."

"He's probably buying, or he wouldn't have come. He's not the type to waste time on something like this without a good reason. I'll have to talk to them at some point."

"Sorry, Ben?"

He blinked and looked at her, and his vision cleared as if he was seeing her properly for the first time in minutes. He sighed. "No, I'm the one who's sorry. I'm not expecting answers from you. I'm talking to myself."

"Talk to me," she invited him, because he still looked stressed and uncomfortable.

It was the same way he'd looked that first day six months ago when Heather had come zooming along in her luxury sports car with her heavy-as-a-brick lawyer's property valuation, and it contrasted too strongly with the relaxed way he'd worked in the garden today, and with the smile he'd worn while he teased Rowena into admitting she didn't like tonight's art.

"I think my ex-wife has found a new man," he said, the

lightness a little forced. "One with assets running to nine figures, while I'm unforgivably still down in the high eights."

"Nine figures?" Rowena turned, finally.

She saw Heather Radford looking like a mix of dynamite and ice in a scarlet dress and a dazzle of jewelry. She leaned on the arm of a man in his sixties who wore his air of authority and success wrapped around him like a heavy winter coat, weighing him down. He didn't look as if he'd laughed anytime in the past thousand years or as if he planned to do so anytime soon. With Ben it was different. Despite the frequently forbidding exterior, you knew there was laughter in there somewhere.

"A hundred million dollars or more?" To Rowie, it was an unbelievable amount.

"That's right," Ben said. "A lot more, in fact. In the wealth stakes, I'm paltry by comparison."

"Are you saying…?" Rowena stopped. She didn't want to get it wrong. Was he really saying that Heather hadn't considered him to be rich enough, with a mere eighty-something million?

"I know," Ben answered softly, as if he'd read her mind. "People are strange when it comes to money, aren't they?"

"They sure are!"

"I will have to talk to them. There's no way out." He was almost talking to himself again. It suddenly struck Rowena that maybe he was still in love with Heather. Was that really possible? A man like this, so successful in so many ways, sighing after the unattainable and refusing to let go?

"He buys art as an investment," Ben was saying, his mouth barely moving. "Usually several pieces at a time, and the gallery needs as many little red Sold dots tonight as we can get."

"But this is a hobby for you, more than a business, Ben, isn't it? It can't be that important."

Heather herself can't be that important, she wanted to say, but that would have been way overstepping the bounds.

"I don't need the red dots for myself," Ben said. "But when this exhibition closes next month, we have a young Hispanic artist coming in whom nobody in the art world has ever heard of, and I really want this lot—" he meant the opening-night crowd "—interested in what's happening with the gallery and willing to come back here in droves to see her work. You'd love it, I think."

He touched Rowena's bare arm but didn't look at her. His attention was directed in full force at his ex-wife, whose gorgeously styled blond hair showed up like a beacon despite her petite size.

"Stay here," he said. "Keep on pretending with the champagne. I'll grab you a new glass. That one's starting to look warm." Deftly he took the stemmed flute from her hand, put it on a waiter's tray of empties and found a fresh one as another waiter went by. "I'll be back."

"You don't have to…"

"Come back? Yes, I do. People are curious about you. Who are you? Why haven't they seen you around? What are the rumors? It's good for the networking."

He wasn't serious, of course. The possibility that he *might* have been serious unsettled Rowena all the same.

People were curious about her? Because of the European designer dress? Because they didn't know who she was? Because of the simple fact that she appeared to be involved with newly divorced Ben Radford, whose charisma left Rowena herself in the shade?

She missed him when he'd left her side.

It was stupid but true. She couldn't help watching his interaction with Heather over the top of her new and nicely chilled champagne flute, seeing the tension and past history between them telegraphed across the large room like signal flags.

Then Heather saw her and recognized her, and Rowena could almost see dollar signs and question marks reflected in her eyes. The questions were pretty easy to answer.

Yes, I'm the Santa Margarita garden consultant you met six months ago. No, I'm not an heiress or a gold digger, but since I'm not romantically involved with your ex-husband, neither possibility should be a problem. Can I go home now?

"Here on your own?" someone said. A male someone, with model good looks and an easy smile.

Rowena didn't like pickup lines and hadn't had enough experience with them to know how to answer. "No, I'm with Ben Radford, who owns the gallery," she answered seriously, not letting herself meet his eyes. "I'm a landscaping and horticulture consultant. I'm doing his garden."

"Lucky Ben Radford."

She *really* didn't like pickup lines. "He does seem to be rather blessed."

"Any chance of yours truly being blessed in a similar way?"

"Um…"

"Your phone number would be a great start."

Okay, she absolutely hated pickup lines. "I can't give you my number. I'm staying at Ben's."

"Lucky Ben again." The guy glanced down at her figure in the gorgeous, revealing dress. "Sounds as if you're *doing* a little more than just his garden."

Goaded, she swept a scathing look in his direction. "You'll never, ever know," Rowena said, with more bite than she'd used in a long time.

Ben himself was on his way back, thank goodness. By the time he reached her, the stranger had sauntered off, leaving Rowena flushed. All right, so she'd managed to get rid of the man, but it hadn't exactly been done with a flourish, and she could have managed very well without his final line, and her own retort, which had left her more flustered than before.

"You okay?"

"Did he buy a whole lot of these metal things?"

They both spoke at the same time. Ben took charge. "Come outside. You look as if it's too warm in here. It *is* too warm in here."

"I'm fine."

"I'm not, though. People are starting to leave. I've talked to pretty much everyone, and I'm ready for a break. Seriously."

He gave a quick glance back at Heather and Rowena understood. He didn't want any more encounters with his ex-wife tonight. Because he still cared that much? Was that the source of the darkness inside him?

"We'll hang around until everyone leaves and then we'll go to dinner somewhere," he said. "We're not due back at Montgomery Field for the helicopter until ten."

He presented it as a decision, not a question, so Rowena didn't argue.

Outside, the air was cool and they found a stone bench in a corner of the courtyard where the exterior lighting was low and the greenery provided a screen between them and the departing art buffs.

"She's thinking about moving east," Ben said.

"Heather?"

"Yes. Sorry. Heather. Not *she*. But there's something about saying a person's name, isn't there, when things have ended badly?" He closed his mouth for a moment, and Rowie could see him struggling with demons that she didn't yet fully understand. "Anyone like that in your life?"

"Yes, and I wish he had a shorter name!"

"Tell me."

"Francesco."

"I guess Jim or Bob would be easier."

"It would get the trauma over with faster, in just one syllable."

He laughed, a soft, ticklish sort of sound that moved his

body a little closer and made Rowena so aware of him she could hardly breathe.

Which was probably why she said it, without pausing for thought. "Are you still in love with her, Ben?" To cure the breathing problem. It didn't work.

"Hell, no!"

"So—" assuming I believe you on that "—why do you find it so hard?"

"Why do you find it hard with Mr. Three Syllables?" he bit back. "Are you still in love with him?"

"No, I'm not!"

"Then why?"

She thought for a moment, resisted the temptation to tell him *I asked you first.* "Because the whole episode was a major failure on my part, and he reminds me of it the moment I think of him."

He shifted on the bench and sighed between his teeth. "That's the problem, isn't it? I never wanted a failed marriage. My parents were miserable together, and then they divorced and for a while that was worse. They sent me off to a boarding school that I hated. And I was determined down to my bones not to do the same thing. But lo and behold, I did."

"Not totally. Because you didn't inflict a horrible divorce on any kids. No terrible boarding schools, no bitter arguments to overhear. You said it to me six months ago—at least you never had kids."

"That's the only good thing I could find to seize on. Still, bottom line, I failed at my marriage. And I hate failure."

"Was it purely your fault? Your failure? I don't believe that!"

"I must have had a share. It takes two. Isn't that what they say? What was lacking in me, that I could never convince Heather that what we had was enough?"

"What was lacking in her, that she couldn't see it for herself?"

"You've gone for the obvious cop-out. Her fault, not mine. But I do think it takes two."

"You're too hard on yourself."

"And you're too easy on me. Don't be, please."

It sounded like an order and she couldn't find an answer to it. All of the options were dangerous.

I'm too easy on you because I'm too interested in what you think and feel. I'm starting to care about you too much, especially when we talk together like this, but you scare me. There's something about you. A place deep inside you that I can't see into, and I think I'm too scared to try.

"Tell me about Francesco," he said, as if he couldn't stomach the silence.

"He was engaged to another woman," Rowena answered awkwardly. "He thought we could have some fun on the side. He was...pretty sexy, pretty practiced at it...and I hated that he could get through my defenses that way. He tried so hard to get me into bed. My body kept telling me all the wrong things. I panicked and ran away. This was Italy. My twin sister married his older brother. I've made a couple of visits there, but I think Gino—my brother-in-law, who is lovely— makes sure Francesco stays out of the way when I'm around."

"Good work, Gino."

"He's a good man."

"So your sister's lucky."

"She deserves to be."

"And so do you. Do you notice how you blamed yourself just now?"

"The same way you did."

"Indeed. For different reasons, I suspect. What did you say about it? *Your* body told you the wrong things. *You* panicked. Your fault, not Francesco's. Why do you doubt yourself so much? Why do you look at me as if you're a rabbit and I'm a wolf, anytime I get close?"

She shrugged. "You said it. I'm a rabbit." Maybe he wouldn't pursue the subject.

He did. She should have known he would. "That's not good enough, Rowena."

"What are you asking me for here, Ben? My life story?"

"That would be a start."

"And where exactly do you want me to start with this life story of mine?"

"Your birth is the traditional place."

"My birth?" She laughed. "Okay, you asked for it."

"I am asking for it, Rowena. It's exactly what I'm asking for."

She sighed. "I was much smaller than Rox. We were born premature and we had this thing called Twin-to-Twin Transfusion Syndrome, if you want to get technical about it."

"I do. Tell me about it."

"Our blood supply was intertwined in the womb and somehow it developed so that I was giving too much blood to my sister and not getting enough myself. It made me smaller. My lungs weren't fully developed and I had a heart problem, too. I got sick a lot, through most of my childhood. I was in the hospital several times with respiratory illnesses, and then I needed some operations for the heart thing."

"*Some* operations?"

"Three. The last one was done when I was ten, which made me a lot stronger, but by then too many habits and patterns were already formed. I distrusted my own body for such a long time. Distrusted its strength and its ability to work the way it was meant to. I probably still do."

She should have stopped there. Ben had received his explanation. She lacked confidence because she'd been a sickly child. Easy. He was nodding slowly as if it made sense.

But something kept her talking beyond the obvious stopping place. "I had to be excused from sports at school, and it made me so embarrassed. The teachers would say things." She mimicked, "'Not Rowena, of course. Rowena's excused.'"

"So that every kid in the class turned and looked at you."

"And I think it wouldn't have been so bad if I hadn't been an identical twin. But there was Rox, such a contrast, bigger and more confident and outgoing, showing me up every time, even though she never meant to. She was the *me* I should have been. Sports, drama, you name it. So confident. She's a great singer. She—"

"Stick to you. I'm not interested in your sister."

"But you can't split us up, that's the thing. Twins are together so much. Their lives and feelings are so closely entwined. And sometimes identical twins stay identical, but sometimes they don't. Sometimes they develop a kind of role separation."

"The shy one and the confident one. Weak and strong. Timid and brave."

"Exactly. And it gets reinforced over time. Roxanna was so protective of me, and without realizing what was happening, Mom and Dad encouraged it. *'Look out for your sister, Roxie. Make sure Rowena is okay.'* So she was always the one to step forward and I was always the one to step back, and if I had a problem, she bailed me out."

"Which made her even stronger and made you doubt yourself even more."

Rowena nodded. "That's how she met Gino. She had to fly to Italy at two days' notice to bail me out because I'd fallen apart over Francesco and couldn't finish the garden project I was contracted to do on the Di Bartoli estate. I was so angry with myself over that. I vowed it would be the last time."

"And was it?"

"Yes. It was really hard, at first, having Rox go to live there. I missed her so much. I still miss her. We talk a lot on the phone. But it's been good for me, too. I can't keep to the old pattern of letting her be the strong one while I sit back being timid and shy. And I'm very happy about that."

"Good," he murmured. "I'm glad."

"I mean, I have a ways still to go. I know that. And occasionally I panic and feel as if I'm back at square one, but then I look at how I was three years ago and can see how much I've…"

She trailed to a halt, realizing how much she'd said.

Ben was looking at her.

The courtyard bench wasn't big enough. If they'd attempted to sit farther apart, he would have had a large, glossy green leaf dangling right in front of his face, so instead the slight scratch of his suit fabric brushed her bare arm, and his jaw was close enough for her to see a tiny patch of skin which he'd neglected to shave.

She waited, watching the way his lower lip had fallen open, and then he said the last thing she would have expected.

"I can see how much you have, too." His voice dropped as a couple came past on their way out. "And I've been meaning to ask, has anyone told you tonight what a great dress you're wearing?"

Chapter Eight

"I was wrong in what I said before, about your dress," Ben said.

"Oh...you were?" The night breeze whipped it silkily around Rowena's legs as she walked from the white limo into the elegant restaurant Ben had chosen. The exhibition opening had been an unquestioned success, with eleven of the twenty-four pieces sold, and strong interest shown by knowledgeable collectors in several more. But his words now made her self-conscious again.

"Yes. I said it was a great dress," he went on. "I should have said that you look great wearing it. It's you, just as much as the dress." He flashed her a quick sideways glance. "More than the dress."

The compliment unsettled her. "You don't need to say that. You didn't need to before."

"Oh, I did!" He turned from her before she could answer, gave his name to the maître d', and they were shown toward a table by the window.

"I'm sorry, then," she said as they sat down.

"For what?"

"For going on too long about my childhood and my health."

"Rowena, how the hell do we get from your gorgeous dress to your childhood health in one single step?"

"Well, I kind of assumed the dress thing was to distract me and shut me up before. Because you didn't need all that detail on my life story as the shy, sickly twin."

"I did need it. I wanted it. It told me a lot about you."

"It's a legacy I'm trying to change."

"Which shows how strong you are," he said with authority. "There are people who'd trade on that kind of thing, and play the pity card. Three heart operations! Good grief! No wonder your parents and sister were protective, and no wonder their protectiveness held you back. Shutting you up was not the intention, Rowena, when I mentioned your dress! The intention was to communicate exactly what I'm telling you again now. You're a bright, attractive woman, made to wear designer dresses anytime you want. Focus on that. Celebrate it."

"I'm trying to. I'm starting to."

"Good. Let me guess, your sister sends them?"

"And shoes. And underwear." Thinking about Rox, she began to relax. "I send her really good books. It's a fair exchange, don't you think?"

He laughed. She always liked it when she could get him to laugh, and she didn't especially like it when he got bossy with her. He let his arm rest on her bare shoulders for a moment. Instinctively she flinched at the unexpected contact, which made him drop the arm and turn on her. "Now, you see? Why did you do that?"

"I— Because I wasn't expecting it, and…"

"Did you like it?"

"I—"

"It was one touch, Rowena. A nice moment, because you made me laugh, and I like laughing, when I remember the fact! My hand is not a loaded gun in your back. One touch is not a binding contract."

"I'm sorry, I—"

"It's okay. Don't apologize." He sighed between his teeth. "I have no right to yell at you."

They reached their table in silence, with Ben's disapproval radiating chills at Rowena's side like an open freezer door.

She'd never had an older brother, but Ben resembled her idea of what older brothers were like. Critical. Intolerant. Zero patience. Absolutely no hesitation in telling you what they really thought about anything you did or felt or said.

It was probably good for her, she decided, lifting her chin. "No, you don't," she told him.

"I'll try not to yell at you anymore, then."

"And I'll try not to give you a reason to!"

Ben saw the stubborn, determined little movement Rowena made with her chin.

Not for the first time tonight.

They'd finished their entrees. To his surprise she'd chosen the spiciest thing on the menu. He shouldn't have been surprised, he realized now. When she wasn't locked in those bad patterns from her past, she had such a zest for gratifying her own senses. He'd seen it in the way she touched things, and in that voluptuous silk nightdress and robe she wore. Of course she would love spicy food.

She'd eaten her meal with unashamed pleasure, and now she was looking at the options for dessert. Their waiter, taking in her very nice figure, had made special mention of the low-fat, low-carb options, and up had come that chin of hers again.

"No, thanks," she said—polite, smiling and steely, all at

the same time. It was a killer combination. "If I'm going to eat fat, sugar and chocolate, I want the real stuff."

"Which one are you thinking of?" Ben couldn't help asking, as the waiter poised his pen.

"The mud cake. À la mode." She gave a cheeky grin.

Ben wanted her, it was time he admitted the fact to himself. He had wanted her all evening, in between the times she made him crazy with her unpredictable backward steps into shyness and panic. He'd never felt like this about a woman before—such an explosive, helpless combination of the desire to take her in his arms and kiss her and the desire to grab her shoulders and scold her as if she were a child. "Now, listen! You don't have to be that way!"

What was he going to do about it?

For the moment, he decided, just keep talking. "So where were we? Favorite nineteenth-century novel?" he asked. They'd already run through favorite movies, bands, travel destinations, exotic cuisines.

"How do you know I like any nineteenth-century novels?"

"Just an inkling."

"Single professional woman with plenty of time alone in the evenings to read long, lo-o-ong books with no sex in them. Is that how it goes?"

"That's not what I meant."

"It's okay, Ben. I'm happy to embrace the stereotype."

"You're not a stereotype," he told her, irritated again.

If she was, he wouldn't be so confused about her, so frustrated by her, so totally unclear as to whether he was going to kiss her at the end of their evening or let her go chastely to her room. He was seriously debating both options.

"In that case," she said, "I'll admit to a pretty obvious preference—anything by Jane Austen."

"Why? Because she's romantic, of course…"

"No, because she's funny."

He was almost certainly going to kiss her, he decided. Unlock the secrets inside her. Challenge her assumptions about herself. Kiss the spice and chocolate from those sensitive lips. Kiss her because if she was unpredictable in her tastes, she was probably even more unpredictable in bed, and it was a long time since he'd made love to an unpredictable woman.

Yes, Heather, that backhanded put-down is aimed at you.

But would he and Rowena get as far as bed tonight?

He looked at her across the table. She took a final sip of her half glass of white wine. She touched her neck with her fingertips—that sensitive place, just below her ear—as if brushing away a crumb or a strand of hair. She'd forgotten about the low curve of her neckline across her breasts, but, oh, Ben hadn't. It was right there in front of him, just a few feet away, shadowed by the restaurant's intimate lighting…

Hell!

He looked up at her eyes and saw the alarm in them just before she dropped her gaze to the thumbnail making its way toward her mouth. "Put that thumb in your mouth and bite off the nail, and I'll cancel your dessert," he growled at her.

"Well, you're the boss." Deliberately flippant. But she added, her tone low and significant, "You're the *boss,* Ben!" How the hell had she read his intentions and his awareness so clearly?

"Yes," he answered. "So?"

She'd looked up at him again, and this time he wasn't going to let her look away. Through the sheer force of his will and her wanting, he intended to hold her gaze.

"Anyway, you're wrong," he said, after they'd stared each other down and both looked away at the same time. "I'm not the boss. You're the consultant, I'm the client. It's a very different relationship. And it's temporary. Which leaves room for it to change."

"It's the only relationship I want. With you. Client and consultant. Nothing more."

Are you sure about that, Rowena Madison?

Her cheeks were flaming. Her eyes had gone dark. She couldn't even breathe properly. Loud and clear, her body was giving him a very different answer. And yet all the doubt was back, too. She displayed the same familiar combination of emotions she had every right to feel and ones she had no cause to saddle herself with, and it drove him crazy all over again.

Final decision made.

He was definitely going to kiss her tonight.

"I'll walk you along to the guest wing." The sound of the departing helicopter formed a backdrop to Ben's words—the same almost menacing throb in the air that had confronted Rowena this afternoon with the reality of how different the two of them were.

"There's no need," she told him.

He ignored her words, and his stride didn't change. He'd gone back to the impatient-older-brother routine—around five years older, probably—and was giving her a duty escort to her suite.

It fit, somehow.

And it was a lot less threatening than any of the other options.

"Got your key? I told Kate to lock everything up since we'd be late." It was after eleven. They'd arrived late back at Montgomery Field and had kept the helicopter waiting.

"Yes, I have my key. You can go. I'm fine, Ben."

"Good," he said again.

Still an older-brother kind of good, she thought. She turned the key in the lock and opened the heavy old door. He waited and she looked up at him, so aware of him after such an intimate, unhurried two hours at the restaurant tonight and after everything they'd said to each other. She was wondering—

Not wondering anything for long.

Not thinking any more about nonexistent older brothers, either.

"Because you really do look fantastic in that dress," he repeated softly, "and I want to find out how it feels against my skin. I want to slide it over your body and then I really, really want to take it off…"

Then he kissed her without either of them getting a chance to say another word.

She didn't want him to kiss her.

She absolutely could not deal with him kissing her, let alone taking off her dress.

At the first confident, unhesitating touch of his lips, a sensation of blind panic swept over her and she fought him, balling her hands into fists and pushing them into his chest, pressing her elbows against the arms that had wrapped with such strength and such certainty around her body.

At the restaurant there had been the awareness, the glances, the possibility hanging in the air like the aromas of spice and chocolate in their meal, and it had panicked her then, too.

Now, when she'd been kidding herself that Ben's attitude was only that of an older brother, the panic was worse and the sensation of lost control more immediate and more complete.

I don't know if I want this, if I can do this or if I should. Give me a chance to find out! Don't crowd me.

But he didn't take any notice of what she wanted. He fought back—seductive fighting, no violence, the hardest kind to resist. His arms grew tighter, his mouth harder and sweeter. He slipped his thigh between her legs, even while her hips were writhing to free herself. She felt the rock-hard, unmistakable shaft of his arousal and that panicked her, too. He was *big*…

He managed to speak, even while she struggled with him. "Hey…hey…Rowena, why are you—?"

"No!" She wrenched herself out of his arms, her body shaking. "No, Ben."

"No?"

"That's what I said, isn't it?"

But she could still feel the tingle on her lips, and the wanting in her whole body. The imprint of his touch and weight lingered on her skin like an afterimage, and she had to hug herself to hide the goose bumps. Such a huge part of her didn't want to say no at all, and wanted painfully to satisfy the almost physical throb of her curiosity. So why was she fighting him? She had no clear idea.

But maybe Ben did...

"That's what you said," he agreed slowly. "I don't think it's what you meant. Not for a moment. Not at all. Not at heart."

"You don't think I know my own mind?"

"No, I don't. Not in this area. Your mixed signals make me crazy. *You* make me crazy, Rowena. I want you, and I think— I *know*—you want me. When I was pressed against you, just now, you gasped."

"I didn't—"

"No, you didn't hear yourself. I did. But I kiss you, I reach up and grab that beautiful promise hanging in the air, and you fight me like a wildcat and it doesn't make sense."

"Okay... Um, maybe it doesn't. I have no answers." She didn't know how to react anymore or what to say. Why hadn't he left? Why was he pushing this? He said she made him crazy, but he didn't seem angry.

"Think about it," he said softly. "Would that make it easier?" He leaned against the open doorway and let his gaze rove over her, setting her alight everywhere he looked. Her mouth. Her bare collarbone. Her breasts. "How about if we just stand here for a minute, while you think about closing your mouth over mine, feeling my body against you, running your fingers through my hair? Think about everything you want, and anything you don't want and get it all clear."

"Ben—"

"And how about we take it more slowly this time? That way, you're the one in control."

For some reason, those were the magic words.

In control.

If *she* was in control.

Acting instead of reacting.

Owning the decisions.

Making the first move…

She was so instantly intrigued by the idea that she forgot to answer him in words. But maybe words weren't necessary. He already seemed to know. There was a light in his eyes, and an expectancy in the way he held his mouth. Oh, that mouth! So smooth and well made and beautiful, in such a male way.

She took several shaky breaths and then she leaned toward him, still tentative, feeling her heart begin to beat faster. This was so new. Feeling the power and the decisions in her own hands. Knowing it was up to her to pull back or go further, whenever she wanted, however she wanted.

Where to begin? What to do first? Was he really saying he wanted her to do this?

Apparently, yes. She couldn't doubt the fire and challenge in his eyes.

She reached out, touched his jaw, then cupped it with a slow, questing caress. He stepped a little closer, as if in response to her hand's command. He was watching her intently, on the alert for her first moment of regret or panic or rejection. So far there wasn't any. When she had the control, she discovered she didn't need the panic, and when there was no panic filling her awareness, there was room for so much more.

She let her hand brush down his neck until she reached the fine cotton of his shirt collar. "Loosen your tie, Ben," she whispered. Would he do it? She waited, breath held, watching him.

He worked at it with a couple of efficient movements until

it hung around his neck. She pulled on it and it slid free. She scrunched it in her hand and pushed it into his jacket pocket, aware of the hard muscle of his chest beneath. "Now the top two buttons." He opened them, and his shirt collar stood open, a pair of white wings against the dark of his tan in the low lighting. "Suit jacket off. I love the roughness of the fabric, but not now. I want something smoother." He nodded slowly, slid the expensive hand-tailored jacket from his shoulders and dropped it on the floor. "Cuff buttons," she commanded.

"Those, too?"

"Maybe I'll want to take your shirt off, or push up the sleeves."

"Whatever you want, Row."

"Mmm. I like the sound of that. Whatever I want."

"What do you want, sweetheart?"

"I'm finding out. Which might take a while…"

"As long as you want. Slow is just fine."

She brushed his neck again, with nothing to get in the way. Ran her hand around to the back of his head and up into the short, slippery strands of his dark hair. They felt cool between her fingers, and they released a delicious, nutty scent into the air.

He smelled so good and so right. The scent of him washed over her skin, surrounding her in a deliciously sensual aura. She stood on her toes, pulled him down to her and rested her cheek against his.

Mmm, so warm. And rough. Softly rough. Just right.

She rubbed her cheek against him, then turned her mouth against his skin. Not to reach his lips, though. His mouth was still three inches away, and she planned to get there in her own sweet time. She kissed the whole distance, bit by bit. No hurry. If it took her ten minutes to reach his mouth, that was okay.

"Say something," she whispered against his skin.

"I can't. I'm burning. You'll find out how much when we get closer."

"That's good enough. You can stay quiet now, if you want."
She held his face between her hands, threading lines of sensation along his jaw with the tips of her fingers.

"I don't know how much longer I can take this, Rowena."
Half whisper, half groan. "I want your mouth on mine so much."

"You need patience. I have a lot more to explore."

"I need your mouth."

"Patience."

"Please…" He laughed, as if hearing the clearly unaccustomed sound of himself—he, Ben Radford, of Radford Biotech and Radford Lateral Enterprises—begging. It actually seemed as if he liked it, because he said it again, on a whisper. "Please, Rowena? Please?"

"Okay, then." She held his face between both her hands and looked at his lips, still deliberately taking her time, making him ache and wait and want for endless seconds.

His lips were soft, smooth, not too full. Not too thin, either. Perfect lips. Perfect to taste. Blurred a little in her vision, because she was so close. She tried them like a morsel of unfamiliar food. One neat touch, the lap of her tongue against the seam. She heard him take in a hissing breath and touched him with her tongue again, a little catlike moment of moisture at the corner of his mouth.

Oh, again.

Deeper, this time. Lasting longer.

"Can I kiss you back now? Please?" he whispered.

"No." She could feel his mouth trembling beneath hers, and a groan of frustration rising in his chest, but found no pity for him.

Let him suffer this a little!

It was such a perfect, delicious kind of suffering.

She kissed and kissed and kissed, breaking off each time to watch his closed lids flicker and his face muscles work in frustration. Each time she returned to his mouth, she went a little deeper, tasting him, melting her mouth into his, then pulling back.

"Rowena, please…" he begged again.

"Yes. Okay. Now. You can kiss me now." The words were painted onto his mouth with whispers of breath, and this time her lips stayed on his.

"Oh, yes, at last!" he muttered.

Seconds later she was drowning in the kiss, lost in it. Sensation charged through her. Ben held her. When he moved his arms against her body, the silky fabric of her dress slipped across her skin. She let her closed eyes drift open and saw his dark lashes almost brushing his cheeks, the glint behind his near-closed lids just a blur in her vision. His face looked younger like this. Very serious. Very intent.

Not wanting it to stop, she pulled him into the tiled entrance of her suite and kicked the door closed.

She was incredible. What had he unleashed?

Ben was too lost in the moment to have any answers. All he knew was that their shared arousal had doubled, tripled, gone off the map, in the space of mere minutes. The whole thing had been so simple. All Rowena needed was to feel the control and the decisions in her own hands and her blind panic fled, as did the distrust of her own body that she'd talked about.

In its place was a passionate, sensitive, questing sensuality that at one level astonished and thrilled him and at another— when he remembered how she responded to beauty and history and color—didn't surprise him at all.

They stood in the entrance of her suite, and he ravished her body with his hands and his mouth. The dress her sister had given her felt even better than it looked—a slippery, swishy piece of fabric that seemed almost alive thanks to the intense life in the body it sheathed.

He slid the fabric up her leg and slipped his hand between her thighs, hooked a strap from her shoulder and found the warm weight of her breast to hold in his hand and to kiss with a hungry mouth. Her body rippled and twisted like a dancer, and her breathing lost its rhythm.

"Oh, Ben," he heard her gasp.

She didn't seem to know where to touch him, but she wasn't letting the fact stop her from finding out. She tried everything. Her hands were like butterflies, like puppies, wandering everywhere, hungry and joyously sensual. They seared down his back, closed over his forearms and pushed his gaping shirt cuffs to his elbows, then ran down again as if she liked the feel of the muscles that were so hard beneath his skin.

What was she doing now? Where were those hands going next?

Oh. Good.

Ohhh, hell!

He was already rock hard and the brush of her hot palm across his trouser fly made him harder to the point of pain.

Yes, please. Oh, yes. *That* kind of pain.

But the contact had gone, as if she wasn't sure about it. He found her wrist and grabbed it, intending to guide her fingers back to where he wanted them, but then he remembered.

Control.

She needed the control.

Aching, fighting the urgency away, he dropped the contact and then felt her follow through on her own. The flat of her hand ran up his fly in a hard, hot press. What was she doing? *Measuring* him? Hell, yes, and apparently she liked what she learned about his generous size. He pushed himself into her palm, aching with need for the skin-to-skin contact.

Instead, he got air. She'd let him go.

But then she grabbed his hips and pulled him against her

body and moved from side to side like a belly dancer, her hips snaking, her breasts sliding across his chest. "Oh, Ben," she gasped again.

"Rowena. Oh, hell, I want you so much."

"Me, too. I mean, I want you. I *want* you." She spoke the words as if she could hear them echoing back in her own head, and he thought she'd probably never spoken them before. Not aloud. Not with such naked intensity. "I want you, Ben."

Oh, glory!

This woman deserved the best lover in the world, he suddenly understood.

She deserved the best, most tender, most committed, most giving, cherishing, passionate lover in the world. She deserved all the promises, all the dreams, all the certainties, and she deserved a man who could give her those things with no hesitation, no complication and no doubt.

And Ben knew down to the marrow of his bones that such a man wasn't him.

The knowledge slugged him in the guts and made him ill, because it led to only one conclusion—a conclusion that he should have drawn hours ago and one that made his whole body burn with suppressed need even before he acted on it.

He had to stop this.

Now.

If he could.

Rowena was plucking at his shirt buttons as if she'd forgotten how they worked. She was laughing at herself, cursing under her breath. "Oh, *jiminy!* Oh, *heck!*" They were the tamest curse words he'd ever heard, but in her state of heightened emotion and need they packed the punch of a street gang cursing out its rival before a fight.

"Hey…" He closed his hand over the fumble of her fingers. "Row, Rowie…"

"Okay, your turn." Still laughing, she took a step back and

he saw that one heaving breast was almost spilling from the top of her dress, saw her mouth darkened and swollen from their kiss, saw the dark glow of passionate sensuality in her eyes.

"Time to stop," he said gently.

The glow went cloudy. "Stop?"

"Yes, don't you think?"

Her answer was an almost feverish glance along the short corridor in the direction of her bedroom. She wanted the bed, wanted the two of them in it, naked and locked together.

So help him, he wanted it, too, enough to make him throb all over, but he made himself say, "Rowena, you didn't even want to kiss me at first. Now you want the whole deal, just like that?"

Again, it was only her eyes doing the talking, all wide and dark and half-blind with her newly and powerfully awakened desire. She didn't understand.

And, hell, how could he possibly explain?

You're too innocent. I'm a jaded wreck. I'd hurt you if we slept together.

She'd slap him in the face for such a patronizing attitude, and he wouldn't blame her for it. Still, it didn't mean his attitude was wrong. It was all true and all too simple. He was jaded; she was innocent; he *would* hurt her. There was a night-follows-day inevitability about the whole thing that made him feel ill.

He couldn't hurt her.

Not this woman.

He couldn't give her what she wanted right now, for the sake of how he would inevitably hurt her because of it later on.

Felt as if it might kill him.

"It's late," he said, and saw the moment when the light left her eyes.

"Okay. Right." She blinked a few times, and touched her hair as if thinking about guiding a strand toward her mouth. "Yes, it is. Gosh."

"Listen—"

"No, no…" She waved away his need to explain, like a society hostess waving away the thanks of her guests.

She didn't understand.

She thought—incredibly, inevitably—that he didn't want her enough, that it was her body and her sensuality he was rejecting. She was going to grab hold of the wrong end of that particular stick and grip it for dear life, with the thorns cutting into her hand until she bled, and he couldn't let that happen.

"You like one-night stands, do you, Rowena?" he asked her, deliberately harsh.

"No! Of course I don't. I—"

"Because that's all it would be, you see. That's the problem here." He saw her flinch and went on quickly. "Not because you're bad at this. Hell! Please don't start thinking that!"

"Then why, Ben? Just pretend I haven't had, you know, my Hollywood cast of a thousand lovers."

"Don't."

"What?"

"The sarcasm. It…it doesn't suit you. A one-night stand is all I have in me, right now, that's all. It just is. For a whole lot of reasons. My reasons. My fault. And you deserve so much more. It would be a huge mistake if we kept going with this. So we need to stop."

There was a frozen moment in which she didn't react at all, like the moment before a jolt of pain from an unexpected blow. Then she nodded, so damn polite and accepting it almost killed him.

"I shouldn't even have started," he said forcefully, trying to get her to understand. A part of him wanted her to yell and scream and throw things. "I should have thought it through."

"You thought at the start that it was only a kiss."

"Yes."

"Who took it too far, Ben?"

"Not you. Not just you. Both of us."

"Why, do you think?" She was hugging her arms around herself now, in an unconscious gesture of self-protection. He knew she'd take his putting on the brakes as a personal rejection, no matter how he worded it, how much he spelled out that it wasn't, or how he tried to soften what he said with the right gestures.

And he didn't have an answer to her question.

Because the right kiss is never enough.

Because I'm a man, and it's been too long.

Because your body came to life in my arms, and it was so perfect I couldn't bear to let it go.

Yeah, that last one. Definitely. That was the answer.

But he was way too horrified by the implications to say it out loud.

Chapter Nine

What was that really about, Ben Radford?

Rowena sank back onto the bed—the one that, for several long, blissful, expectant minutes, she had thought she would be sharing with him tonight.

All night.

She knew now that he still wanted her. Her body sang and tingled with the imprint of him, with the smell of him, with the unmistakable signals he'd given off. For a few moments she'd read him wrong and her old doubts had come flooding back, but in hindsight she knew what was genuine and what wasn't. Men didn't pretend about that kind of thing. They couldn't, even when they tried. The evidence was there, right in front of them. Right against her own body, hard and demanding.

But despite the strength of his desire, he'd slammed on the brakes so hard she could practically hear them squeal, and he'd talked about one-night stands. Did she like them? Because she was setting herself up for one, right there.

That's all I have in me, right now.

The words repeated in her head, the way certain other words of his had repeated in her head six months ago.

Thank heaven we never had kids.

The two statements were connected. She could hear it. The same depth of emotion. The same raw truth. The same fears for the future. The same half-hidden pain.

She sat up slowly and caught sight of her own reflection in the beautiful antique cheval mirror. Her hair had tumbled down from her head and onto her shoulders. Her black dress was twisted around her body and had slipped low, showing the lacy edge of her strapless black bra and the swell of breasts that seemed fuller than they had been this morning. Her lip gloss was long gone, but the color of her mouth hadn't changed. It was a dark, sensual pink from the effect of Ben's kiss.

She didn't look like herself.

Because she wasn't herself.

Something had changed in her tonight—one of those moments of discovery and growth that, sure, you lost a little ground from at some point, but you never lost it all. Three steps forward and two steps back.

She'd talked about it with Jeanette, and Jeanette was right. You never went all the way back to how you were before, when the forward step was like tonight's had been. It was too powerful and too important.

She said to the mirror, "This is not about you, Rowie. Remember that!"

He hadn't rejected her because she was sexually inept, or painfully needy, or primly unsure, or any of the things she'd been in the past and never wanted to be again. This was about him. His divorce. His hurt. His doubts. The changes he needed to make.

True, understanding all this didn't exactly make Rowie want to jump for joy. She didn't for a moment believe that anything she could say or do would have the power to make him any different. He had to find his own answers, the way she had to find hers, and she knew there was a huge chance that he never would find them. Not everyone was interested in that kind of quest.

But it gave her a strange kind of peace.

Because for once she didn't blame herself.

For a woman crawling with intense, unsatisfied desire, she somehow managed to sleep very well, and woke up on Friday morning hungry to work on Ben's garden.

Ben reached out and shut off his computer screen with a frustrated click of his tongue. He didn't want to hide away in his office when the sky was so blue outside, and when he wanted to see what Rowena and her crew were doing.

No, forget the damned crew! He just wanted to see her, because he'd been avoiding her, thinking that was best, but he couldn't stop himself from wondering how she was holding up after last night's near disaster, when he'd gotten so close to taking her to bed. How much had he shattered her fragile new growth?

It was around three-thirty in the afternoon and he'd kept himself locked away all day, cloaking his own awkwardness and regret about last night in the convenient disguise of urgent, important work.

Everyone bought into the urgency without question, of course. Kate tiptoed in with coffee every forty-five minutes until he had to tell her to stop. She tiptoed in on three other occasions with handwritten questions from Rowena, each of them noted meticulously in indigo ink on a sheet of her letterhead stationery, as if he might have forgotten that Madison Garden Restorations was currently under contract here.

After seven hours of this, he couldn't take it anymore—
not so much the interruptions, but his own sense that he
needed a good chance to read Rowena's face. When he arrived
outside, he found Pablo and Wayne packing their tools away
and Rowena sitting on an old water barrel scribbling notes as
if her pen couldn't keep up with her thoughts.

She didn't see him at first, and just kept scribbling, head
tilted down and face invisible beneath the baseball cap she
wore. Immediately, despite his best intentions to keep at a safe
distance, he wanted to touch her. Hug her and feel her cheek
against his chest. Touch her sun-heated hair and feel the warmth
against his palm. Rediscover the contrasts in their two bodies.

And he wanted her to look up in his direction, but she
didn't. Not even when he knew she'd seen him. She was pretending. Her body had tensed a little. The pen paused on the
notepad and began tapping while she pretended to think.

"What's happening?" he said, to force her to lift her face.
"Are you stopping?"

"It's nearly four o'clock and we started at seven." She
smiled. It was careful and a little tentative, but genuine. She
looked…at peace with herself.

So she was okay, then.

Hmm.

It took him aback, and he realized he'd read her as being
more vulnerable than that. She even looked as if she'd slept
well, which he sure as hell hadn't. He told himself he was
relieved that he hadn't destroyed something new and precious
inside her, but then he had a flash of honest and utterly male
ego. Damn it, had she shrugged off the power of last night that
easily? Was the power all in his own misguided head? Was *he*
the one who—

What? He had no idea.

"I wanted to finish early," she was saying. There was a slight flush in her cheeks. "I need to catch my breath a little over the weekend and do some thinking about what we do next."

"Catch your breath?"

"Mentally, I mean. I'm going to head out to a couple of plant nurseries and landscaping supply places now, and visit the Mission San Luis Rey tomorrow, look through my reference books, start refining my ideas. You said it would be okay for me to drive your SUV."

"Tomorrow I'll drive you," he offered, without giving himself a second to think it through or question his own motivations. "You can show me over the mission and tell me how it fits into your thinking."

After one telltale beat of silence, she told him, "Sure. It would be good to have your input for that."

"What time do you plan to leave?"

"Whenever suits you. Midmorning?"

"Sounds good."

The pen tapped on the notepad some more.

"Rowena, about last—"

She cut him off. "If this is going to be some kind of morning-after speech, Ben, you don't have to, okay? If you're going to tell me it was a mistake, and that it's you not me, and all that stuff, seriously, please don't. We said it last night. We got as far as we're ever going to get on the subject with talking. We're done. We're okay."

She smiled at him again, and it was obvious that she meant it and wanted him to leave. He nodded, and echoed the word she'd used herself. "Okay…"

Were they really? It seemed as if they shouldn't be. But somehow they were.

Ten minutes later, he heard her start up his SUV for her landscaping supplies reconnaissance trip, and when she came back just before dark, she disappeared into her own suite and ate her dinner there, brought by Kate on a tray. Ben didn't see her until she came tapping at the door of his home gym room at ten-thirty the next morning, wearing jeans, a strappy little top and an alert, busy expression.

"I'm wondering if you still want to come to the mission, Ben, and if the timing still works for you." Rowena had prepared the query in advance, to give Ben an easy out if he wanted one. He probably did.

A part of her wanted him to take the easy out, too, but there was a stubborn element inside her that *didn't*—the element in her that was clearly a sucker for punishment.

Seriously, though.

She'd done the avoidance strategy last night, hunkering down in her room and surfing the channels on the TV, eating Kate's delectable homemade Irish meat-and-vegetable pie, whose light, flaky pastry had gone soggy from the steam beneath a metal dish cover during its journey from the kitchen. Like the soufflé the other night, the spoiled pastry reproached her for taking the easy way out.

Eating in her room reminded her too much of her own past. She'd spent too much of her life hiding and running away and opting out. If she avoided Ben instead of learning to deal with her attraction to him, where were the steps forward?

"The timing is fine," he said. "Just give me five minutes. I'll meet you outside."

She waited by the SUV, not knowing if he'd want to drive or relax in the passenger seat. He'd given her his spare set of keys and told her to keep them while she was here. When he appeared, he had his own keys in his hand. "Jump in," he told her. "I already know the route. Got your notepad?"

She held up a daypack. "And my camera."

"What are we looking for?"

"Shapes, colors, design details I can make reference to in what I do at Santa Margarita."

"Make reference to?"

"Kind of echo. The shape of an arch, or the carving on a door. There are some things I'm going to have custom built—like a new gate for the side entrance, because the old one is beyond repair—and I want to get the designs for those done next week."

She was going to stop there, but he kept asking questions and he was the client so she answered them, which meant that they talked the whole way. They spent almost an hour and a half at San Luis Rey. It was nearly two hundred and forty years old and you could literally smell the history—old wood and incense and cool adobe and countless other scents mingling together.

Rowena loved it, the way she always loved things that were old and beautiful and created with reverence and care. It was great that Ben had come with her, too, because it gave him an input that really helped her. Their feet crunched over the old stone and clay, and she lost count of the times they both pointed to the same detail at the same time.

"Tell me what you love and what you don't, Ben," she said. "Whether it's the layout of a garden bed or the scent of a flower, anything."

He did as she'd asked, and came up with some very individual likes and dislikes that she wrote down and incorporated into her thinking until her mind was crammed with new ideas and imagined vistas. In a job she loved for almost all its varied phases, this was maybe her favorite part of all, when the ideas came flooding in after she'd seen so much beauty made by others.

"We'd better get lunch," Ben said, when they turned out of the mission parking lot. "You must be hungry after all that. It's almost one-thirty."

"Kate can show me where the sandwich fixings are. I'll be fine."

"You'll be fine," he echoed on a drawl. "Me, I can't wait that long. We're going to eat. Sushi okay for you?"

"Oh, I love sushi! It's like eating abstract art."

He gave a crooked, half-secret grin, as if there was something very amusing about that statement, and as if he'd somehow *known* that she'd say something funny about eating sushi, and suddenly the awareness that they'd managed to forget about—or that Rowena had managed to kid herself about—for most of the morning was back again.

On the driver's side of the SUV, he seemed too close. They'd shared some good times together this morning. They'd agreed on a lot of things. Laughed with each other. Taken pictures of each other standing in front of flowering cacti and moss-covered stone.

She *liked* him too much when they relaxed together like this, the way they'd done over dinner on Thursday night, and she didn't want to like him so much, because the liking didn't make the wanting any easier.

For one long moment she came very close to bailing on the sushi. She could insist that he take her back to Santa Margarita right now. She could claim she wasn't hungry, after all, and elect to take a nap in the car while he ate.

No, Rowie, remember? No running away.

So she ate sushi across an elegant little table from Ben, confronting the fact that every minute she spent in his company seemed to dig her in deeper, and as yet she had no strategies in place for digging herself out again.

Chapter Ten

"Hey, what have you found, Wayne? Oh, wow, and it's not broken! It'll be beautiful when it's cleaned. Want to do that? You know the drill, right? Soak it first. Come see this, Pablo."

Ben paused in the concealing morning shadow of the veranda and watched Rowena and the two men at work. The past six days had passed by too fast. She was going back to Santa Barbara tomorrow to put together a detailed portfolio of her garden plan, while Pablo and Wayne completed the work she'd set for them. She would be back in early October to oversee the next stage of the process.

There had been some amazing changes at Santa Margarita over the past eight or nine days since her arrival, not just in the tangled mess of garden itself but in the men, too. Somehow, Rowena's totally unselfconscious enthusiasm for every sensory and historical detail of this place had infected them like a fever, and they were as happy as she was when they found some old Spanish coins, several handmade farm tools and the sturdy wooden bucket that had once dipped into the well.

It reminded Ben of what had happened the first morning Rowena had spent here, six months ago, when she'd shown him the brilliant crimson cochineal pigment within the powdery white crustings on the cactus leaves.

How did she do it? How did she open up such magical new worlds in a man's perception without having the slightest idea of what an exceptional woman she was? Ben had had the strangest feeling over the past few days, whenever he found himself straying outside to watch or take part in the work— a sense of stretching and renewing himself, like a rattlesnake shedding its skin.

After brooding so much on his failed marriage, analyzing his part in it, looking for where he was to blame, he was so ready to think about something else, and that something turned out to be…not so much the garden project, because he was pretty good at focusing on his projects.

No, this felt different. It *was* different. There was no structure to it, no plans or goals or agendas. He simply saw and felt and lived—everything from the acid-like roughness of the dirt on his hands, to the yawning blue of the sky, to the sound of some unknown bird trilling from its secret hideaway in the jungle of cacti.

Sometimes he liked what was happening to him, sometimes it gave him a kind of vertigo.

Rowena wasn't the only one who was scared of her own power to change.

Now, apparently, Wayne had found an intact ceramic bowl, with just a chip or two out of the rim, and was showing it to Pablo and Rowena. All three of them were peering at it intently, smiling at it, holding it up to the light, tracing with reverent fingers the traditional patterns in the glaze beneath the masking layer of dirt.

Ben strolled out into the sunshine, and Rowena looked up from Wayne's discovery and saw him.

"You're supposed to be stopping," he told her. He was having people to dinner tonight and he wanted her there, not skulking in her room eating her dinner off a tray the way she might be tempted to do. He liked spending time with her, loved watching her blossom and hated it when she hid herself away.

Rowena had changed since she'd come to Santa Margarita, and he had an almost possessive interest in the process, which he didn't want to examine too deeply. He couldn't afford to have a woman like this one get under his skin when he had so little to give, and when he so dreaded another major failure and mistake.

"I have nothing to wear," she'd protested two days ago when he'd issued the... Okay, Ben, don't call it an invitation; be honest and call it a command.

"So, go shopping," he'd told her. "Buy yourself something new. Add the bill to your cost estimate for the garden."

She could tell it was a challenge, and he'd seen the familiar lift of her chin. There was an electric charge in the air this week every time they talked. Sometimes he knew it still terrified her, but more often, now, she mentally rose to meet it. He wished he had it in him to do more to reward her effort, and he had a strange idea that she understood more about him than he wanted her to.

"Not sure if I can take time off to shop," she'd said about the shopping trip.

"Pablo and Wayne would be deeply wounded to know how little you trust them."

"Oh, I do trust them! They're getting so involved in this garden!"

"So leave them to it, and go buy an outfit. You don't need to get your hands dirty anymore. I want to see those garden plans printed off your computer in full color, not the dust under your fingernails."

"My fingernails will be fine with ten minutes' work, but all right, on Friday I'll stop at lunchtime," she'd promised two days ago, and lunchtime it now was.

The men had their instructions for the afternoon. Wayne showed Ben the newly discovered bowl, guiding him with proud gestures and broken English through its best features as if he'd made the darned thing himself.

Rowena was brushing the dirt from her hands. "Before I stop to eat," she said to Ben, "I want to walk you through what I'm thinking and hit you with some questions."

"I said yes to the fruit trees, yes to the Spanish-tiled fountain, yes to the barbecue modeled on a traditional wood-fired oven. There's more?"

There was definitely more.

Rowena wasn't sure how she was going to bring up the issue, however. It had been nagging at her for days, an undercurrent of ill ease beneath all her satisfaction at how the project was going and beneath her simmering awareness of Ben.

It all harked back to that moment during her first afternoon here over a week ago, when she'd sat on the crumbling old wall at the far reach of the garden, closed her eyes, dreamed her vision of the garden and heard children laughing and the thwack of a ball.

Barbecue grill area, fountain and fruit trees, yes, cacti and wildflowers, plants native to California and plants introduced by the Spanish missionaries, herbs and paving stones, yes to all of that, but the garden needed something else.

It cried out for it in her heart.

The garden needed a place for kids, but Ben had never mentioned it. She knew he had an older sister in England with children. She didn't really know how he saw children fitting into his life. How did she ask him something like that when she'd heard what he'd said about his childless marriage?

She led him past the cleared space near the house and out to where that old wall still baked in the sun. She didn't plan to take it away or restore it, because it fit just the way it was, almost looking as if it had grown out of the earth. It would be a perfect backdrop for brightly flowering native plants. Meanwhile, to the left of the wall, at the rear of the house's eastern wing, there was an open space…

"I've been wondering about this section," she said, gesturing to the space and the background vista of the mountains.

"It's a blank canvas right now."

"Yes, and I'd like to put a grove of citrus trees along here." She gestured and walked as she spoke, and Ben followed her. "With an opening through to the vista of the mountains beyond." Her plan ran to more detail than this, but he would see that later on in her computer-generated sketches. "But over here, I'm not so sure."

"Tell me the options."

"A rose garden is a possibility, or…do you think you'll ever have kids here?" Why had she phrased it that way? It sounded too ambiguous, too personal. She went on quickly. "Visiting kids, you know. Nieces and nephews, or the children of friends. Because I'm wondering about a playground. Swing sets and a sandbox and a fort. And a baseball diamond. Even a tennis court."

He didn't want to think about it. She could see the resistance building moment by moment. "My sister and her family visit maybe once every three years. By the time they come here next, they'll be too old for playgrounds."

He didn't want to consider the possibility of kids—the possibility that he'd ever become a father himself—because that would imply that he might marry again and he was too cynical about marriage now. Once bitten, twice shy of the whole institution for the rest of his life. He'd made that very, very clear.

Disappointed, hearing the phantom echo of those laughing children again in her head, Rowena let the subject go. But the imaginary children refused to accept her decision. They insisted on the reality of their own existence and kept on laughing, kicking a ball around, splashing and shrieking.

Splashing.

Walking with Ben back to the house, she wondered about that.

Splashing.

Could she convince him to put in a swimming pool? Kind of sneak the idea past him without him understanding the possibilities it opened up? Because people could change. She believed that.

A pool wasn't remotely traditional, but she wouldn't site it in the traditional part of the garden. It would have its own space, walled on three sides in an echo of the three-sided veranda that was part of the main house. A fourth side would be made by that grove of citrus trees she wanted.

And then if he ever changes his mind about having a family of his own...

The kids would have somewhere to swim and play—space in the sun, cool shade, sparkling water, the scent of orange blossom wafting nearby.

The prospect made her feel so much better that she had to laugh at herself. What was she doing, feeling good about finding a play place for dark-haired, bright-minded Radford children who didn't yet exist and probably never would?

Never?

Yes, never.

Because she knew Ben's cynicism was real.

It wasn't going to vanish just because she wanted it to.

Still, when she added the pool to her computer-generated

plan, she would make sure it appeared as a seamless part of the design so that he would never guess who the pool was really for.

Those kids.

She was allowed to imagine them if she wanted to!

In her suite she showered and changed, scrubbing the garden-stained nails Ben had commented on. She munched down the turkey-salad sub that Kate had left for her on a tray and drank a glass of juice. Then she went to the mall to buy the kind of outfit she could wear to dinner tonight with Ben's high-profile guests.

Channeling her twin, Rowie knew that gray professional business suits were not in the running, but changing a lifetime of timid shopping habits was hard. She spent the next two hours fighting a mental battle between her outgrown need to hide her body and her new determination to be different.

Different, how?

Dress sexy? The hot pink satin slip dress and the strapless crimson sheath looked so overdone, and the fabrics felt metallic and full of static cling. Dress safe? The black trouser suit made her think of bad business meetings, or the funeral of an unloved great-aunt. Dress like a bridesmaid? The ball-gown styles were too formal, and she and strapless just did not get on. Dress down? Cotton florals were for picnics. Jeans—even designer jeans—were plain wrong.

She wished Roxanna was here…and then she was glad Roxanna wasn't.

I have to do this myself. I have to do it for me, not for Rox or Mom or Ben or anyone else.

Me. My fingers. My eyes. My love of beautiful things.

Suddenly Rowena wasn't thinking about styles and conventions anymore, nor about her own body and its history of illness, the heart and lungs that hadn't work properly for so many years. She wasn't even thinking about the thin, silvery scar down the center of her chest from her long-ago surgery, that she could still see in the mirror sometimes, in the right light. She was only thinking about texture and color and line, the way she thought about those things in a garden, the way she thought about them when she chose vintage silk and lace designer nightwear purely for her own pleasure.

How come she'd never made the connection before?

She went into a designer boutique with her senses on high alert as they were when she went into a garden, and fell in love with about a hundred shapes and color patterns all at once. The store was already having a fall sale, bringing some of the prices down to a point where she only winced rather than gasping.

The gasping she saved for the silky textures and unusual silhouettes, the color combinations she would have put in a garden but never on her own body. And yet they worked. She tried on three stunning cocktail-length dresses and could see for herself in the mirror the truth in what the sales assistant told her. "It looks great on you."

She made her final choice on the basis of price—yes, the least expensive of the three—and knew Rox would laugh at her, but *some* of your longtime safety nets you had to cling to in this scary and uncertain world, right?

She'd always been budget conscious, and she had no intention of adopting Ben's suggestion to add the cost of the outfit to her bill for the project.

Even though she still had to buy matching shoes....

It was five-thirty in the afternoon by the time she got back to Santa Margarita, and Ben's guests were due in an hour.

Ben's guests were also much more numerous than Rowena had realized they would be. Somehow, she'd imagined, oh, say, four couples, with herself and Ben bringing the total to ten. And she'd been busy in the garden this morning and absent at the mall all afternoon, and hadn't seen Kate's frenetic preparations or the catering staff who'd arrived to help create a five-course Friday-evening meal for twenty-four.

They arrived by limo and sports car and helicopter and SUV, and the elegant living and dining rooms of Ben's beloved Santa Margarita were soon crowded and humming with noise. Busy with greetings and introductions and business conversation, Ben couldn't stay at Rowena's side, and she didn't expect him to.

The first guests had already begun to arrive when she appeared from her own suite, and when he paused briefly in front of her to say, "Here's your favorite camouflage," as he handed her a bubbling glass of champagne, he didn't mention her new dress.

But he looked at her.

A lot.

All evening she noticed it, which she wouldn't have done, of course, if she hadn't been looking just as much at him. Why was it so significant when two people's glances kept meeting that way? The pull was physical and real, and the sense of secret, shared delight was powerful and good.

Ben liked the dress. His eyes said so, even if he didn't actually say the words.

This has never happened to me before.

No, it really hadn't. She'd never known how it felt to have a man's awareness following her through a crowded room, crossing to her over a laden table, cutting through laughter and conversation, bathing her in a sense of warmth and happiness for hours, making promises…

She didn't know about the promises, though.

Maybe those were only in her own head.

Meanwhile, most of the twenty-four guests were too curious for Rowena's comfort as to who she was and where exactly she fit in Ben Radford's life.

One woman seemed to know. After they broke from the long dining tables for coffee and chocolates, a dark-haired, designer-clad and impossibly thin and well-groomed woman named Jennifer Sable came up to Rowena and looked her up and down, taking in the new dress with its striking color combination of pale gold, pale blue, coral and cinnamon brown, and the pale-blue strappy shoes.

"Oh, yes," she drawled. "Dr. Madison, the garden expert. I've heard about you from Heather. Ben's latest project." She smiled at the last possible moment, making Rowena wonder if she'd only imagined the disdainful subtext.

"That's right," she smiled back. "I think we're both very happy with how it's going."

"Good for you. Nearly finished, I'm thinking." Another sweeping look, this time upward, at Rowie's freshly styled hair.

"Oh, no, not at all!" Hadn't Jennifer glanced through the windows, before darkness fell? "We've only just started. There's a long way to go."

"In that case, I'll expect an impressive result." Another smile flashed out, and Jennifer's cool fingers rested for a moment on Rowena's arm, as if to say, *We're friends, really, aren't we?*

But Rowena didn't think that they were, nor that they ever would be.

She felt Ben's touch on her shoulder and didn't flinch the way she would have done a week ago. Instead, she turned to him in relief and told him with a surprising amount of truth, "I'm having a great time."

One bitchy friend of Heather's, apparently married to a business associate of Ben's, didn't have that much power over her spirits anymore.

Not when Ben Radford kept looking at her with that slow-burning fire in his eyes.

* * *

The evening went late. The last of Ben's guests didn't depart until midnight, which made Rowena feel like Cinderella, suddenly, because the party was over and she was going home to Santa Barbara tomorrow. The fact that she was coming back again in a few weeks' time wasn't good enough.

Ben met her by the big wooden door leading out to the veranda, after he'd seen off the final departing car. "Go to bed, Rowie." He'd begun to call her that, the way Roxanna often did.

"I am." She eased out of the door Ben had opened for her.

Even though she didn't want to. It was foolish, really. She'd barely had a chance to talk to him tonight, and she wanted him to say something about her dress. He would probably never see it again. She wanted a whole lot of things from him. What was it about midnight? What was it about the promises you could so easily imagine in a man's eyes?

"Your flight's at nine, isn't it?" So, not the dress. Talking about her travel plans just didn't deliver the same satisfaction. "I'll drive you in," he told her, stepping onto the veranda, also. The night air had cooled to a perfect, balmy desert stillness after the warm, late-summer day. "I'm playing golf tomorrow, quite near the airport."

"So we'll need to make a fairly early start."

"Want Kate to wake you with breakfast?"

"No, I'll set an alarm. I'll eat at the airport or something. She's earned a sleep-in."

I want to kiss you, Ben.

Rowena was standing there, stringing out their conversation with meaningless detail about her plans for the morning in the sad hope that his eyes might go cloudy and dark and he might reach for her. Yes, reach for her with unmistakable intent softening his mouth and filling his face, because she wanted him to kiss her and it was very, very simple.

Suddenly, astonished at her own rashness, she heard

herself say it out loud. "I want to kiss you." Not with a stammer. Not with a question in her voice. Loud. Clear. With the rock-steady certainty of a child announcing a need for candy. "I really want to kiss you, Ben."

He went still. She saw his brow tighten and his eyes narrow. He looked tired. He looked as if something inside him hurt. But then he gave a tiny nod, stepped forward and leaned down. He touched her cheek with his closed mouth, like a brush of warm fabric briefly in contact with her skin. "There you go," he muttered. It hardly counted. It was gone before it even started.

"No."

"Oh, hell, Rowena!"

"Yes, it has been, a bit." She lifted her chin and met his suffering look head-on. "Tonight. This past week. Hell, I mean. Not kissing you again after that first time. It's my last night. I...I'm really aware of that."

"You'll be back." He leaned his elbow against the wall and turned his head, masking the upper part of his face with the heel of his hand, as if he didn't want her to see him wince with pain.

"Will you kiss me then? In October?" She reached up and circled her finger and thumb around his wrist, needing to see him.

He let her pull his hand away from his face, didn't shake off the contact when their hands fell to their sides with her fingers still ringing his wrist. "We can hope the need has worn off by that point, can't we?" he muttered.

"You can hope that. I don't." She touched his face, let her thumb brush over his lower lip, and remembered last week when he'd given her full control and she'd learned so much about how to touch a man, just in the space of those long, precious minutes of exploration and discovery.

His jaw felt a little rough, like the floaty raw silk panels on her dress, but his lip was full and smooth and he smelled of chocolate and coffee and wine. Would he taste that way, too?

She leaned into him and stretched up, wanting to reach his mouth. It looked so good, three inches away, three inches of burning, intoxicating air. She tilted her face, lapping her lower lip with her tongue.

"Rowena, are you trying to seduce me or something?" His voice dropped low and rumbled in his chest. "Did you have too much of that champagne?"

"No." She ran her fingers down his chest, feeling the movement of his breathing beneath the butter-soft cotton fabric of his shirt.

"No to the seduction?"

"No to too much champagne. Half a glass. And a few sips of wine. To the seduction…I…I think so. Yes. I think I am. Trying to do that." His mouth was such a distraction—everything about him was a distraction—she could barely string her sentences together.

He sighed between his teeth, looking down at her, refusing to touch her, clearly suffering. "You don't know what you're asking."

"Poor little me," she said, mocking both of them. "To understand so little about these things."

"Stop it…" He stroked her hair back from her forehead and brushed his thumb across her cheek.

"Stop asking you to treat me like a grown woman who knows her own mind?" Again she brushed his mouth with her fingers.

"Maybe you do know yours—a lot more than you did. You're changing, Rowena—but you don't know mine. No." He shook his head impatiently. "That's wrong. You do know it. Because I've told you. I'm burned. I'm scarred. Angry. *Difficult,* damn it! Bloody impossible, in fact. You don't need a man like me."

"No?"

He dropped his voice. "You don't, Rowena. You need a man who can make promises, and I have no promises left."

"You made promises to me all night, tonight. I saw them in your eyes."

"Those weren't promises, they were—" He stopped. Apparently, he didn't know what they were.

"Anyhow, you can kiss a woman without promises, Ben."

"Not you."

"Why not me? Why am I so different?"

I'm not different, said her body. Feel me, I'm a woman like any other. I want. I give. I ache.

"You are really asking for this, aren't you?"

"Yes."

He groaned and swore, shifting his body forward so that the adobe brick beneath his shoes made a gritty sound. "I'm not taking you to bed. Just so you know." The final word lost itself against her mouth.

Chapter Eleven

Just a kiss. He wasn't taking her to bed.

Because he didn't want to hurt her.

Ben wanted Rowena to be in no doubt about the fact of his desire. She was going home tomorrow for three full weeks, and if she went with the sense that he'd rejected her, he'd never forgive himself because he knew how much it would hurt her.

And yet, at the same time, if she went home with expectations—rosy, pretty ones about romantic dinners and nights of lovemaking and a sure future when she returned again—he'd never forgive himself for that, either, because he knew he couldn't follow through. Not when his sense of failure and bitterness about his marriage still burned in him so much.

So, just a kiss.

One deep, long, fabulous kiss.

It would say what he wanted it to say. It would stop right there. It would be safe.

But there were a few things he hadn't figured on…

Hell. For a start, she felt so good in his arms. She tasted so good. All chocolatey and sweet and warm. Deliciously unexpected at a point when you thought the evening was almost over, like a midnight dessert buffet.

She was *soft*—female soft, gracefully soft, responsively soft. Her mouth gave beneath his, opening for him. Her stomach and her breasts pressed against him. Her hands cupped and touched and stroked, with a sensual curiosity he knew she'd only begun to discover in herself.

After a while—already too long, way longer than he'd intended—Ben mastered his growing hunger and tried to ease away. But she wasn't having that. No way in the world. She grabbed his face between her hands and pulled him back to her. Her mouth stopped giving and became the taker, the plunderer. She didn't speak, didn't even acknowledge that he'd tried to stop.

He opened his eyes. He couldn't remember closing them, and it felt like such a surrender to have done it.

Take me. Possess me.

That was what a pair of closed eyes said. How the hell could he let himself say that to any woman? The implications daunted him and made him want to run a hundred miles.

Her eyes were closed, too, her lashes sweeping her flushed cheeks, her face relaxed, every muscle and every nerve ending given over to the flood of her desire. Who would have known she had such a powerful, responsive sensuality?

He *should* have known. There were so many clues in the way she ate, the way she laughed, the way she stopped to touch a flower. But he'd been blind.

And of course he could stop this.

Of course he could. He hadn't seriously tried yet, that was all. A few firm words from him would do it. Any moment now, he'd say them. *That's enough, Rowie. Go to bed.*

But for now…

Why did he love her dominance so much? How was it even possible for her to dominate him? She was so much smaller, so much more finely built, so much less experienced or sure of herself as a lover, and yet for once in his oh-so-self-directed life, she was the one calling the pace and the tune.

No. *He* had to stop. He had to.

"Rowena…" His mouth moved against hers as he said her name and she captured his lower lip between her teeth, nipping him gently then licking the tiny moment of pain away.

She didn't answer. Her hands fell to his belt, unbuckled it and whipped it out of the fabric loops. He thought she would throw it aside, but she kept it and used it, looping it around his waist and then sliding it up his back to chest height. She pulled it tight and close, anchoring him against her body…against her breasts and hips and soft belly…and then she kept kissing.

"That's better," she whispered.

She's going to seduce me.

This was the second thing he hadn't figured on—that Rowena had no intention of stopping this or of letting him stop it, no matter what he did or said, no matter what promises he didn't make, and how she might feel about it in the morning.

She's just not going to let me put on the brakes.

The realization was instant and electric. It slammed into Ben like a runaway truck, and his desire surged.

Which was the third thing he hadn't figured on—that he would want her in-control seduction so much and that he'd be so painfully aroused by the very thought.

All right, he *had* to stop.

"Don't you dare even think about it," she said, as if she'd read his mind. Or maybe the momentary tightening in his body told its own story. Her breath was hot in his ear.

"Do you know what you're doing to me?"

"I hope so." She began to lead him by the belt looped around his back, taking short, easy steps back as she tugged him forward along the veranda in the direction of her room.

"Hell, you're *planning* this!"

"Planning is one of the things I'm good at…"

"Rowena—"

"I'm not going to beg." In the meager light spilling from inside the house, her eyes were so dark and big they were like cave pools, and she didn't take them away from his face for a second. She had that belt pulled tight, which made her knuckles graze his sides and her breasts push into his chest. "I want to beg. I want to say please sleep with me tonight, Ben, but I'm not going to. And there's this other part of me—" she laughed "—that wants to tie you up with this belt, your wrists behind your back and another belt around your ankles, and give you no choice, but I'm not going to do that, either."

"No?"

Shoot, he was almost disappointed….

"If you really want to stop this, then stop it. You know I don't have any real power over you. But feel the way I want you." Deliberately, she snaked her body against him, rocking her hips against his aching groin, pushing her breasts forward, driving him wild with need. "See how far I'm prepared to go. And believe me."

"Believe you," he echoed.

"Believe I'm only thinking about tonight, and that's enough." She stood on her toes and kissed him again—one sweet, short *smush* against his mouth, like offering him a ripe, juicy peach and then snatching it away again. "Believe that I just want this now, Ben Radford, no matter what happens in the morning."

He practically began to pant, while she smiled a we-share-a-wonderful-secret sort of smile that melted his bones like fudge in the sun.

Okay. Okay. What more could a red-blooded man do? Who was she kidding when she said she didn't have any power? Right now she had all of it, cradled in one hand, and that was fine by him.

"Let's go, then," he said, his voice scratchy with need.

Rowena's room was dark, but the shutters and drapes were open and the moon was bright. Ben's skin looked almost silver where the moonlight hit and dark where it didn't. It was darkest of all at his groin. She stroked him there, amazed at how satiny and how big he was. He shuddered at her touch, grabbed her hand and signaled, *Harder!*

Hard was good.

All of this was good, but she knew it would be difficult in the morning.

And she didn't care about that.

Let me have this one night. Let me believe in my own power to deal with whatever happens afterward. Let me know that for once this was my decision, something I want, something I'm doing with my eyes open.

Or shut.

She liked them shut, too, because then her other senses took over so strongly. She could hear the frayed, rushing sound of Ben's breathing, the tear of the foil packet he opened, and the slip of the rumpled sheets as they moved. She could smell the complex mix in the scents filling the room. Clean linen and old wood, soap and shampoo, coffee and chocolate, woman and man. She could touch him and taste him. Silk and salt and sweetness.

He pulled her on top of him. "If it's the control you want…"

"I want everything."

"Just tell me. Tell me if anything's not right."

"So far it's all perfect."

He kneaded her backside, ran his hot hands up her spine, pulled her down and closed his warm, wet mouth over her nipples, one and then the other, sucking her and circling her with his tongue, sending shots of aching hunger straight to her groin.

Oh, this was most definitely right…

Filling her, he rocked his hips back and forth, but even though he pushed deep inside her, it wasn't enough like this, with her legs straddled at his thighs. She wanted more, wanted him closer.

She stretched her legs down and felt herself tighter around him, closer to him, the closest she could ever be. His mouth was still on her breasts and his hands on her bottom. He squeezed her against him and kept rocking into her, chasing her mouth so he could kiss her, burying his face between her swollen breasts, pushing against the sensitive mound and groove at the core of her body, breathing like a steam train, rocking and pushing and—

The powerful climax took her completely by surprise, snatching her up and sweeping her away to a place she barely knew existed. She grabbed on to Ben's body anywhere she could, needing an anchor, something to connect her to the world, because otherwise she might never come back from this wonderful, hypnotic kingdom.

Those cries, were they coming from her own mouth? She heard him groan and felt his body begin to convulse like hers, and as her own climax began to ebb she felt his as a second wave of pleasure breaking over her, just as intense as the first.

It seemed to last for so long, and even when it was over, there was no sense of loss or sad completion. He was still here, wasn't he? He was still touching her, kissing her temples where the hair had grown damp, holding her tight as if he couldn't get enough of her body or her taste or her smell.

"Come here," he whispered raggedly.

"I'm here already, aren't I?"

"Come closer. Lay your head against my chest."

"I'm not too heavy for you?"

"Are you kidding? But slide off, if you want. I can still hold you that way."

"I'd love that…"

"So would I."

So she pillowed herself against his heart and heard the beat of it begin to slow. She *owned* that heart, right now. Not for long. Just for tonight. But she owned it because she was the one who had made it beat faster. Now it was slowing, slowing. It made her sleepy. And happy. Very. Too sleepy to think.

"Okay?" he whispered.

"Yes. Perfect."

"Good." He sounded drowsy now himself.

She fell asleep in his arms.

She didn't know what time it was later, when she woke to feel him easing himself out from beneath her. Skin slid across skin, slow and quiet as a mouse, and she was left with only the warmed sheets against her leg and arm instead of his body there.

He thought she was still asleep, she could tell, and he didn't want to waken her. He moved almost silently in the room and she kept her eyes shut, listening to the faint sounds as he found his clothing. She thought about speaking and opening her eyes, letting him know she was aware of him leaving. Hey, Ben…

But, no. It was best if he went now, best if he thought he hadn't disturbed her. She didn't want any awkward words going back and forth, and she didn't want him still here in the morning, making distant, tight-mouthed excuses for a hasty scramble from the room.

Much better this way.

Then she heard the door click shut behind him and the difficult part started.

She had known it would start at some point, but knowing didn't help. And so soon, too. It was like physical pain. Your head knew it was coming, but your body couldn't prepare. Expected or unexpected, it felt just as bad.

She rolled over and looked at her clock. Almost four-thirty. He'd stayed nearly all night, wrapped in her arms. And she hadn't set the alarm. She reached out and did so, then spent the next ninety minutes looking at the numbers on the clock change, and never got back to sleep.

At six, after a quick shower, she found the belt she'd wrapped around his body discarded on the floor.

"When you come back..." Ben began, in the middle of an airport commuter terminal crowded with weekend travelers.

Rowena turned. She had a little time before her flight so she was buying coffee. Her neat fingers were wrapped around the lidded paper cup and she was dropping her change into the black leather purse dangling by a long strap from her shoulder. He hadn't picked his moment very well.

And he didn't even know what he was going to say.

When you come back, we'll leap right into bed and I want you to be wearing the black lace strapless bra and please do that thing with my belt again.

When you come back, I'll make sure I have business in another state and we'll communicate via fax or possibly Morse code, or even smoke signals if we have to, because we don't actually want to connect face-to-face.

Something along those lines, anyhow.

"It's okay," she said, easing her way through the cluster of people waiting to be served. "I know."

"You do?"

"Things will have changed. From last night. You don't have to spell it out. Well, you already did spell it out. Before. The one-night-stand thing." She began to sip her coffee, while they found a tiny island of space where they wouldn't get bumped by cabin luggage carried past in people's hands. "I have no expectations, Ben."

He winced inwardly. Okay. So she did know. That was really what he'd needed to say, even if he'd temporarily forgotten the words, and now she'd said it for him—that she couldn't afford any expectations.

They'd had a one-night stand.

She looked…oh, hell…so brave and resolute about it, not as fine and dandy as she wanted him to think, but not falling apart, either.

"And we can still be friends," she told him gently, as if she was the one drawing the line in the sand.

At which point he made the unlikely discovery that, as well as being stronger than she thought, she was also a survivor. Even when she got knocked down, she got up again. Maybe not with a bounce and a grin but with something more enduring than those things—a slow, quiet, unstoppable grit.

"I guess…"

"Of course we can! We'll have a lot to talk about, with the garden." She smiled at him—cautious but warm—and took another neat sip of her coffee through the hole in the plastic lid.

"True," he conceded.

"So is it a deal?"

"Is what a deal?" His head felt thick this morning. Too little sleep. He'd lain awake for hours while Rowena slept with her head pillowed against his heart, wondering about how unforgivable he was for having taken her to bed.

"That we're still friends," she said.

"Is that what you really want?"

"It's what I'm shooting for." She gave another sweet, determined smile. "So, deal or not?"

He had to laugh. "You're really pushy sometimes, aren't you?"

"I'm learning to be."

"Okay then, it's a deal. We're friends, Rowena Madison."

She actually reached out for his hand to seal the deal with a shake, and when their palms and fingers touched it felt too familiar and good. He knew what her hands could do. And he liked it. Felt bereft when the handshake ended and the contact stopped.

He watched the way she drank her coffee, studying him thoughtfully over the top of the lid. "Can I ask you something?"

"Sure," she said.

"Do you see a therapist?"

"Um, yes. Why?"

"Just wondering."

They didn't have much time. Why had he picked now to probe for more about her life? Around them, people were looking at their watches, talking on their cell phones, saying things like, *Yes, I'm in the terminal now.* Ben himself had several of his management VPs already waiting at the country club for him to show up for their scheduled Saturday golf and corporate bonding. He should leave.

But he didn't. "And is he the kind of therapist who's still looking at what happened to you when you were five years old, after you've already been seeing him for fifteen years?"

"She. No, she isn't. I love Jeanette. She's very practical. We set a goal, and when we both feel I've achieved it, we set another one."

"What have some of your goals been, so far?"

"Oh, let's see." Another sip of her coffee. He couldn't help watching her mouth, and the way it pouted against the white plastic. "Being able to buy a new car without my dad coming with me, and without visiting each car yard about fifteen times. Being able to go back for a second shot at a radio interview about historic garden restoration, when the first time I hid in the bathroom. The producer was really nice about it—

apparently a lot of people get nervous on the radio—but I was so angry with myself for ruining their schedule."

"Goals as concrete as that."

"Some of them aren't so concrete."

"Tell me."

Being able to handle a one-night stand. Was that one of her goals?

He had a brief, ridiculous fear that maybe he was just a deliberate, short-term experiment in her life. He had so little faith in anything like this now, so little faith in relationships, that it almost seemed possible.

Ben, you're being an idiot. Does that sound like Rowena's style to you? A few words from her, and you'll regain some sense.

But she only gave an enigmatic smile. "I have to have some secrets, Ben." And he so badly wanted to kiss her goodbye that he had to put his hand in his trouser pocket to hide the evidence.

At that point came the first call for her flight.

"I won't see you for three weeks." It sounded, so help him, almost *whiny.*

Fortunately, she gave the comment a professional interpretation. "I may well have the plan and budget put together before that. I have some other work commitments so I can't come down any sooner, but I could courier you the plans if you want to see them sooner."

"No, it's fine. Bring them in person. I'll have questions."

"And tweaks?" She smiled again, as if she knew him too well.

"Those, too, probably. There's no sense in us faxing each other back and forth about it. We'll wait."

For three whole weeks.

They said their goodbyes, and the issue of body contact or no body contact was resolved by the fact that she still had the coffee in her hand, while her purse strap began to slide off her shoulder and she had to slide it back up.

"See you soon," Ben said inadequately.

"Three weeks." Another smile.

He left the terminal, because the risk that he might say something about the strapless black bra and the leather belt was becoming too great. The rest of the day stretched ahead as dry as the summer dust that could sweep over Santa Margarita in a July wind, and he had the sick-making realization that he was in way deeper than he wanted to be.

And yet he knew it could never be deep enough.

They'd agreed to be friends—hell, it was a weak word, sometimes!—but she deserved so much more.

Great performance, Rowie.

It had been a performance for herself, not for Ben, and it was the kind of goal that Jeanette might have set her. Being able to say goodbye to Ben Radford at San Diego Airport without crying or stammering or saying totally the wrong thing. Without dropping to the floor and wrapping her arms around his knees. Without spoiling last night.

That was the most important part.

Putting her bags in the car, driving away from Santa Margarita, checking in at the terminal and saying goodbye to Ben, all of it without spoiling or losing or messing with last night.

And I did it.

The knowledge got her through the next three weeks and its typical schedule. The weekly sessions with Jeanette. Shopping and laundry. Coffee with a couple of new friends. Phone calls to current, future and prospective clients. Hours of work with garden reference books, computer screens, budget spreadsheets and large-format color printers.

Then it was time to return to Ben's ranch.

Which was when she discovered that she'd been kidding herself…a little bit…or maybe quite a lot…about how well she'd handled their one-night stand. Despite everything she knew about Ben and all the things he couldn't promise, despite the friendship they'd agreed on, her heart wanted more.

Chapter Twelve

"I have the whole order on standby with each of the suppliers, ready to go as soon as I phone it in," Rowena said.

It felt strange now, to speak in this formal, practical way to Ben, when just a few weeks ago she'd yelled at him, laughed with him, whispered in his ear, made X-rated demands of him in the dark. But she'd had plenty of practice at using businesslike language with other clients, so she managed it and he made no attempt to challenge her performance.

In fact, he managed the businesslike language, also. "You mean everything? Down to the last pot of herbs and bare-root tree?"

"Everything. They know there may be some tweaks."

The two of them had the large-format landscaping plans spread out on the table in his office at Santa Margarita, and Ben had gone through the whole of the large bound portfolio containing her sketches, budgets, lists of plants and numerous other details. They'd been here for nearly two hours on a Monday morning, after she'd driven down from Santa Barbara in her own car yesterday afternoon.

He hadn't kissed her. Not last night after they'd eaten one of Kate's four-course date meals together in the dining room. If Kate was hinting something, she had to stop! And definitely not this morning, when everything had been so very business-like. They hadn't come within three feet of a kiss.

They'd barely even touched, and Rowena knew why.

Because of the whole nothing-to-promise thing.

Because they'd agreed to be friends, and friends didn't kiss.

They'd had a one-night stand, and Ben couldn't follow through with anything deeper, so she'd pushed for friendship, he'd agreed and he was making sure to stay well away and keep all the right boundaries in place.

Which was good, because when she thought of all the promises she wanted a man to make to her one day, and all the boundaries she wanted him to break down, she didn't need the pain of giving her heart to a man who never would.

"And they also know we may wait on it for a few more days if you have more extensive changes you want to make," she went on, talking about the garden plan.

"No, but I like it. I like all of it very much," he said, leaning on his hands over the conference table.

Rowena couldn't help watching those hands, strong and tanned, with their fingers spread to support part of his weight. The hands, the squared wrists, the muscled forearms below the rolled sleeves of his business shirt. She knew them very well, she knew his whole body, and yet she had no claim over it.

The wanting hadn't gone away. She still struggled over the fact sometimes, as she'd known she would. There were days when she felt she couldn't handle it and made a panicky decision that she would never attempt to get involved with a man again. But there were more days in which she couldn't regret what had happened.

It had changed her, and the changes were good ones. She felt stronger, more sure of herself as a woman. She understood more about the power of her own heart, and about what she wanted from life.

And somehow, despite all the reasons why it shouldn't be possible, she and Ben were friends.

You couldn't consider something a failure if you'd gained a friend from it.

"Even the swimming pool? You like that, too?" she asked him, dragging her focus back to where it belonged.

On Ben's garden.

"If you'd asked me in the beginning if I wanted a pool, I'd have said no, I can swim at my gym in the city, but the way you've done it is so good. I really liked the sketch you made of it beckoning through the citrus grove. You're good at drawing, Rowena."

Friends did give each other compliments, sometimes.

"You mean my computer is," she corrected him.

"I'll concede that your computer helps, but there's something about them that could only have been done by you. You've convinced me on the pool, and on everything else."

"If you don't want any more time to consider, then, I can get on the phone. We don't want to push the planting phase back too far into the colder weather."

"How long will the phone call take?"

"Not long," she told him, "since each of the suppliers has the full order on hand and is just waiting for the official go-ahead. Ten minutes? Deliveries should start arriving tomorrow, and I have the extra work crew starting then, too, under my full supervision."

Friends were pleasant and polite to each other, when discussing practical arrangements.

"So today's your only free day?" Ben asked.

"I guess."

He leaned lazily on the table, let his gaze meet hers for a moment, which, very carefully, did not last too long. "Want to come riding, then?"

"Riding?"

Could friends go riding on a sunny October day?

"You've seen the horses," he said. "Riding is what they're for. And they need it. Pablo and Wayne take them out sometimes, but not often enough. They're getting lazy and into bad habits. Kate's threatening to take riding lessons but I somehow don't see her as a horse person."

"What makes you think I'm a horse person? I've barely been on horseback in my life."

"I like watching you go outside of your comfort zone," he drawled, and she started to blush when she thought of all the ways she'd done that in his company.

Riding a helicopter, attending an art opening, wearing seductive dresses and sliding a belt around his chest to pin him against her body. Did she even have a comfort zone anymore where he was concerned? Did she want one in any other area of her life? Would she know herself with such a new degree of freedom?

"The pinto mare is very gentle," Ben was saying. "She won't throw you when she gallops."

"I am *not* galloping!"

"Aha, but you are riding, then."

"You tricked me into that!"

He only laughed, then added, "Kate can put a picnic together for us. You'll manage in jeans, and there's a box of riding boots in the storeroom. Hats, too, if you want the full cowgirl effect."

"I guess I'm getting it, whether I want it or not."

Forty minutes later, they were ready to go.

* * *

If Rowena could set herself goals to reach, then so could Ben.

Goal number one. Follow through on his promise of being friends with her, since it was one of the few promises to a woman that he still knew how to make.

Or thought he knew how to make.

Riding across the glorious, mountain-shadowed sprawl of his ranch, he wasn't so sure. He was looking forward to their day together too much, and he itched to touch her. Not just to kiss her, but to brush his hand across the rear end so nicely packaged in a pair of age-softened jeans, to drop a hand around her shoulder and give her a squeeze when she made him laugh.

All of that was more than friendship, but nowhere near as much as a woman like Rowena would ultimately want, and nowhere near as much as she deserved. She deserved a man who loved her and trusted her and trusted himself one hundred percent. She deserved a man who could make promises instead of mistakes. She deserved marriage, with everything that a good marriage meant. Children and laughter and plans and sharing.

And the prospect of failing if he attempted those things quite simply paralyzed him. Marriage was the only thing he'd ever failed at in his life—the biggest mistake amongst a huge litany of successes—and if he never married again, he couldn't fail at it a second time, so he was safe.

He knew all this, but knowing it didn't help him to change.

Rowena went ahead of him on Bonnie, the pinto mare. At first, her pose in the saddle was stiff and unsure. She turned in the saddle to throw panicky looks at Ben roughly every ten seconds and gripped the reins as if she expected Bonnie to take off on a steeplechase at any moment.

But then, as they left the home field and went through a swinging metal gate, he gave her a few pointers. "Keep your heels down, give her a pat when you're pleased with her." And he watched with pleasure as the familiar transformation began to unfold. She was getting used to this, and she was starting to like it.

"I'm pleased with her so far," she called back to him. "She hasn't thrown me off."

"So give her a pat, nice and firm. If you're too gentle with them, it tickles and they don't like that. And she's not going to throw you off. I'll keep a lookout for anything that might startle her."

He watched Rowie lean forward to pat Bonnie's neck with a nice solid thwack. "Wow, she feels so warm!" She grinned. "And her coat is softer than I thought. It's like satin. Is she enjoying this?" She thumped the mare's neck some more with the flat of her hand.

"Yes, and she knows what it means. That you like her."

"Oh, I do! Well, I'm starting to." Her hips rocked slightly, in time to the mare's sedate tread as they walked along.

"I can tell."

He could always tell, with Rowena. It was like the light changing after rain, like dawn breaking over the mountains. She began to smile. Her body softened. Even her voice dropped in pitch and went more musical, instead of that high, nervous flutter it went into sometimes. She looked around her with curiosity filling her face, instead of doing the deer-in-the-headlights nervous stare.

She got imaginative with leather belts, and didn't notice when the neckline of her dress scooped lower....

"Want to go faster?" he asked, because he needed the distraction.

"That's like changing gear in a stick shift, right? You do something to the controls, and then suddenly you're going zoom."

"Kind of. Their gaits are very distinct."

"Except, in this case, where are the controls?"

"Kick her sides with your heels. It won't hurt her. She's a wall of solid muscle."

"And then when I want to slow down again?"

"Sit back a little, squeeze on her reins, but don't yank too hard. She has a good, responsive mouth."

"Mmm, on second thought, I don't think I want to go faster."

He didn't push her on it, and they kept to a walk for an hour until they'd reached one of Santa Margarita's far boundaries, where grazing land shaded up into the lower slopes of the mountains.

It was time to eat.

He dismounted and tethered his own gelding, Grasshopper, to a scrubby-looking tree whose botanical name Rowena could no doubt tell him in Latin, then turned to find her still perched up on Bonnie, clutching her mane and looking down at the ground as if she considered it very, very far away.

"Just take your right foot out of the stirrup and swing your leg over and down," he told her.

"Mmm, it's that word *swing* that's giving me trouble. My hip is telling me it's too seized up to swing, and if I lean forward onto Bonnie's neck, won't she buck or something?"

He went up to the mare. "Do you hear that, Bonnie? She thinks you're going to buck. Can you believe she'd make such a catty comment about a born lady like you?" He switched from crooning horse voice to human talk. "I'll hold the reins. And then I'll hold you. It's fine if you lean on her neck, and I can step you down the last bit to the ground."

Rowena nodded, and he could see her squaring up her resolve. He had to smile at her clumsy dismount...but then she arrived in his arms with a Bridget Jones kind of yelp, her shapely butt pressed into his groin, her arms bunched awkwardly between the saddle and her chest, and her legs sliding against his.

At that point everything changed.

Ben wrapped his arms around her, feeling the weight of her breasts nudging briefly against his tightened muscles. He could smell the fresh, delicious scent of her—hot cotton and fragrant soap—and with his head turned to the side, his cheek rested for a moment against her back.

"Here you go," he said, and lowered her the final foot of distance to the ground.

And suddenly he wasn't smiling anymore.

He was aching.

In all the wrong places.

In all the very worst and most impossible and not-according-to-the-friendship-agreement places.

Which were also the exact places a man most liked to ache, when he knew there'd be the right reward at the end of it.

He wanted to keep her here in his arms with the horse's satiny side behind them. He wanted to turn her around to face him and push her against the saddle leather with the sheer force of the passion in his kiss. He wanted to find a soft place in the earth and spread out the picnic blanket and make love to her out in the open air until they both burned.

"We'd better start on that picnic," he muttered, because he knew there was only one appetite he could permit himself to fill right now, and it wasn't the one that clawed deep in his gut. Finally—*finally*—he managed to let her go and turn away from her.

How the hell was he going to get through the rest of their ride? How the hell was he going to handle her time at Santa Margarita without taking her to bed again? And how in the world could friendship feel so nice, and at the same time so totally unsatisfying and inadequate and wrong?

Friendship be damned, he wanted her so much, and the only feeling inside him stronger than the wanting was the determination not to hurt her with his lack of anything more to give. His fingers were knotted with stress as he unfastened the buckles on the saddlebags, and he was glad for the chance to keep his back to Rowena while he mastered his own control.

Kate had packed a couple of carrots and apples for the horses.

Ben took them from one of the saddlebags and gave them to Rowena without looking at her. He was apparently very busy with the rest of the saddlebag contents. "Here you go. One each. Keep your hand flat so they don't accidentally crunch on a finger at the same time."

"Right. Sure," she said brightly. "I can do that."

She should have tried harder to climb down from Bonnie's back on her own. It hadn't been *that* far to the ground, and her hips hadn't been *that* stiff. It sort of seemed appropriate that it was because of her sheer clumsiness that she'd ended up in Ben's arms for that long, difficult moment.

It had ruined the mood. He was frowning now, looking distant and preoccupied and not meeting her eye. He was probably thinking what a wimp she was, not even willing to trot and then not brave enough to get down from the animal on her own.

Or else he thinks I did it on purpose so he'd have to put his arms around me and—

And nothing.

The moment hadn't gone anywhere. It had lasted too long and yet still flashed by too fast. Frozen with the unexpectedness of it, she'd just had time to feel the breath leave her lungs and the blood start to beat in her veins, and then the awkward bit of body contact was over.

They were friends, and friends didn't stand beside their horses in the sun and kiss and whisper and hold each other as if the world was about to end.

Let it go, Rowena.

The horses crunched down the carrots and apples in about ten seconds and then stood dreaming in the sun and occasionally making little whickering and snorting noises to each other—possibly the equine equivalent of, "Get that fly off my back, couldya, please?"

Ben and Rowena sat on a warm, dry rock and ate mini spinach quiches and mini tomato-and-goat-cheese tarts and about six other kinds of intricately created mini things that, as Rowie had noted, Kate always seemed magically able to produce at short notice whenever finger food was required.

"I thought we'd be having peanut-butter-and-jelly sandwiches," she commented, because the horses seemed to be talking more than the humans right now. "Tiny ones, of course."

"You're right," Ben said. He smiled—crooked, brief and reluctant. What was he thinking about?

Rowena kept trying. "With a side of tiny, tiny sour-cream-and-onion chips."

"And tiny, tiny bottles of cola."

"And it's not that I don't like tiny food, but sometimes you really want to open your mouth wide and take a big, chewy crunch, don't you?"

"Especially on a picnic." He seemed to be relaxing a little, finally.

"Yes, I think that's the problem," Rowie answered. "We need to give Kate some feedback on her ideas about picnic food. Especially horseback picnic food."

"Do you like the horseback part, though?"

"My hips don't. The rest of me thinks it's wonderful."

"You'll have to work on the hips, then, so we can do this again. Do something that gives them a stretch and opens them up. Take a dance class, or…" Ben trailed off, with a sudden hitch in his voice.

"No other ideas, Ben?" Rowie teased him lightly, not quite sure why he hadn't finished. "Just the dance class?"

"That's about it." He still sounded a little strained. "Dance class. But not tap. Something more…" He stopped again.

A silence fell.

Again.

Broken only by the breeze and the polite, friendly horse conversation. "My reins are tickling my neck. Could you nudge them for me? Thanks."

And Rowena finally realized what Ben's problem was. They'd been talking about opening up a woman's hips, and she could think of a really good way to do that, but you needed the right man for it.

She needed Ben.

She wanted him, and he wanted her, and they weren't talking about it or acting on it, because they were *friends,* not lovers, and it was one of those elephant-in-the-room things. The elephant right here on this rocky mountain slope, lazing in the sun with the horses, making the air thick with its invisible, unspoken presence.

"Not much of an ideas man out in the sun," Ben said eventually. "It's making me sleepy or something."

"Want a tiny, tiny chocolate éclair?" Rowena asked, peering into a container labeled Dessert as if she was a scientist peering at the results of a critical lab experiment. That way she didn't have to meet Ben's eyes.

"Sure."

Ten minutes later they were back on their horses, picking their way down to the track that led beside a dry gulch in the direction of the ranch house. The horses seemed still half-asleep, clopping along in a lazy rhythm.

"This is driving me crazy," Ben said. He'd barely spoken since they'd begun to ride again, and now his voice was tight. "I want some speed. I'm going to canter him for a bit. Do you mind? I'll wait up ahead there, where the fence angles off to the right, and you can catch up with me."

"That's fine, Ben."

He kicked Grasshopper on, and the dark, golden-brown animal broke into a canter, leaving Rowena and Bonnie behind, and the human in the partnership horribly aware of how inadequate she must seem to Ben, when she wasn't prepared to go beyond this sedate, boring walk. How about if she at least tried to trot, the way he'd suggested earlier?

She gave an experimental nudge with her heels against the horse's sides the way Ben had told her to do and Bonnie picked up her pace a fraction. She nudged harder, and Bonnie decided that she was supposed to copy Grasshopper and canter, too.

Which was a lot faster than it looked.

Rowena forgot about pulling on the reins to make the horse slow down. She was too busy clinging to the saddle so that she didn't fall off. Ben was already way ahead, the sound of Grasshopper's hooves on the dirt masking the sound of Bonnie's quickened pace behind him. He reached the angle in the fence, wheeled his horse around and stopped to look back to see where she was.

Rowie had enough spare brain space to realize that he'd seen her plight now, and was coming back to help, urging his own horse into some impressive speed, but most of her attention was fixed on the fact that she was going to come through this situation with a degree of dignity and guts or seriously die trying.

Pull on the reins, Rowena. Get yourself upright enough and stop grabbing on to anything you can reach and just tell this pretty girl that you want her to stop. It's just a misunderstanding. She's really not trying to kill you.

What had Ben said? Heels down? Squeeze her mouth don't yank on it.

He was already halfway back to her, his silhouette dark against the backdrop of bright sun. Rowena couldn't have seen his face at all, even if she'd had time to look. She managed to get her backside more deeply in the saddle and her feet angled right in the stirrups, then she squeezed on the reins and Bonnie dropped into a bouncy trot that was in many ways scarier than the canter, and then, thank goodness, a loping walk.

Ben reached her. "What happened? I can't believe she bolted!"

"She didn't. We just got our wires crossed. I wanted her to go a bit faster, and she thought she was supposed to go a lot, *lot* faster and catch up to her friend. It wasn't her fault."

"You did well to stay in the saddle. I can't believe that, either, to be honest. Hell!"

"All right, Ben, you can say it. If I'd let you teach me to trot and canter properly before lunch, I would have known what to do."

"I don't need to say it. You just said it for me." He hadn't cracked a smile yet. Was he angry with her?

I don't care. We're friends. Friends can take each other's anger every now and then.

"How did it feel?" he added. It was casual, but forced.

She recognized something, suddenly. "Ben, were you scared for me?"

"Bloody terrified."

"Sorry."

"You haven't told me if you liked the speed."

"Oh, right. You know what? When my adrenaline settled down a bit, it felt great." She grinned at him, and watched him press his lips together as if something had given him a massive headache and he just wanted to go home.

When they arrived back at the ranch, she gave him her inexpert help untacking the horses and he barely spoke. Just the odd necessary instruction. "Don't pinch her when you pull on the girth strap. Make sure she knows you're there, anytime you're around her back legs. Grab that saddlebag and bring it inside, could you?"

As soon as the saddles and bridles were hung on their racks and the horses were turned loose onto the grass, he disappeared inside, leaving Rowena to follow in his wake. She felt let down and out of spirits as she took the saddlebag of picnic remnants into the kitchen.

Kate was there, already in the process of whipping up something fabulous for dinner. "Is he in his office?" she asked, because there was only one *he* who mattered around here, and that was Ben.

"I think so. I'm not sure."

"Would he want coffee, d'you think?"

"Oh, gosh, Kate, I don't know." Rowena sighed.

And Kate wasn't stupid. Or inclined to stay quiet when she had something to say. "You two have an argument or something?" She moved her comfortable figure around the kitchen as she spoke, and picked up a spoon to stir a sauce that smelled of mushrooms and wine.

"I...I don't think so. But he does seem angry. I know I scared him."

"Scared him? For heaven's sake!"

"Or my horse did. We had a communication breakdown and she went too fast. He'd gone on ahead, and when he turned back and saw me kerfloundering along, he—"

"Kerfloundering?"

"It's a technical term. I *felt* like I was kerfloundering."

"And he what? Got angry right at once, like? Or did he get angry later, because he'd been scared?"

"That."

"Hmm." Kate poked a fork into some boiling potatoes. "You have an opinion on this."

"I'm not sure that you want to hear it, darlin'."

"Oh, I do!"

"Mr. Radford's not very good at being wrong."

"Well, it's not something that happens very often, from what I can work out."

"Exactly! So he's not used to it. Would be better if he got a little more practice."

"So he…?" Rowena prompted.

"Runs away if he sees it coming, like Henny Penny thinking the sky is falling."

Rowena laughed out loud. "Kate, I'm sorry, but that is the most inappropriate, unlikely comparison, when you have Ben Radford in the equation."

"Isn't that right? But it's true, all the same. You know it yourself, I think. You're getting to know the man pretty well. The good and the bad and the ugly."

"Not much ugly."

Kate gave her a sideways glance. "No, not much. He's a good man to work for." She paused, which gave her last words more significance.

"And that's what we're both doing, you and I. Working for him. That's all we're doing." Rowena understood, speaking it out loud.

"Best remember it," Kate said mildly. The mildness belied the hidden strength behind the words.

Good advice. More than that. Almost a warning.

Chapter Thirteen

Somehow, after the ride, they managed to keep to the friendship thing with no more getting it wrong or breaking the rules or confusing the situation. No more Rowena forgetting what Kate had told her to remember, either. She could thank the garden for that.

By means of Rowena working long, outdoorsy days that started early and finished late, as well as the distraction provided by the enlarged work crew and Ben's sudden immersion in business matters that Rowena didn't even try to ask him about, they kept to the professional working arrangement and the friendship agreement.

She returned to Santa Barbara for a few days' work on other projects at times when the work at Ben's could progress without her involvement. She came back to the ranch for the last time when the plants and trees began to arrive, and late on a Wednesday afternoon on a mild sunny day in early November, the garden was finished.

"Not that a garden is ever finished," she told Ben, as they stood on the veranda together. "It's always a work in progress. It will still be unfolding years from now, as the trees and perennials grow."

"I'm looking forward to it."

"Some things you'll have to thin out eventually. And no matter if you take all the care in the world, a couple of plants always die and need replacing. The plans show exactly what's been put in where, so you'll know what to buy."

"Would you like some photos, occasionally, for an update?" He wasn't looking at her, and she wasn't looking at him. They both looked out at the garden. Rowena was so aware of him. His strong body acted like a magnet, pulling on her, drawing her closer. She resisted the pull, the way she'd been resisting it for weeks.

"That would be great," she answered him.

"I'll get Pablo to send some."

"Great," she repeated, less sincere this time.

Ben Radford was a busy man. She shouldn't feel it like a slap in the face just because he didn't intend to take the photos and send them himself.

"And I've listed alternative choices that are suitable for the same position," she went on, "if there's something you turn out not to like."

She could hear the wistful note in her own voice. She always hated this part of a project—the part when her own involvement came to an end. And if she'd hated it in the past, she hated it a hundred times more because this garden was Ben's. The lengthening afternoon shadows creeping across from the western wing of the old adobe house underscored her shadowed mood.

"I'm going to hire someone," Ben told her. "A qualified professional gardener, who can make sure Pablo and Wayne do the right things."

"I can give you a list of people in the area," she said. "I've heard a few recommendations from landscaping suppliers and plant nursery people."

"Can we take a walk through it? I can't believe you're telling me it's finished. All the trees are in? Even the pool is filled?"

"Yes, even the pool is filled. We trucked in a couple of tankfuls of water so it wouldn't take days to fill with a garden hose, and the pool company put in all the right chemicals this morning. I thought you'd want the full effect right away."

She had come into his office at the ranch and summoned him a few minutes ago, and they were both standing on the veranda looking at the garden as if they didn't know what to do next, while the hired crew packed away the last of their gear and Pablo and Wayne tested the computer programming of the irrigation system.

She expected Ben to move off the veranda and start exploring, but he didn't. He seemed reluctant, for some reason. Distant. Holding the whole conversation at arm's length, the way he'd been holding Rowena herself at arm's length since the day of their ride. "Wow," he murmured, still standing there, just looking.

"I know. The whole crew was great, so gung ho to get it done fast and right. Too gung ho, a couple of times. When we found that flour grindstone, Wayne practically took a bullet for it, as if it was the president and he was on security detail, because the other guys thought it was a plain old rock and wanted to chip right through it. He threw himself into the hole, yelling, 'Not just rock, not just rock,' and look at it now."

Okay, stop rambling, Rowie.

"He's right, it's not just a rock," Ben said. "It's beautiful."

"I know. I love it." It was a big, worn piece of circular pale-gray stone with a sinuous, pinwheel-shaped groove in it, where the freshly ground flour had once gathered. Having been rescued from an irrigation pipe trench, it now sat like a piece of sculpture, the centerpiece in a rockery filled with native Californian flowers.

"Word's going to get out," Ben said. "I've already had a couple of business associates asking about you—if you take on garden design that doesn't have a heritage component. In particular, Alex or Jennifer Sable might give you a call."

Rowena remembered Jennifer from Ben's dinner party two months ago. Unfortunately, you couldn't afford to be too picky about the personalities of your clients.

"I haven't done much of that kind of thing," she said. "My academic background is in horticultural history. But what I have done, I've loved."

"I'll have friends wanting to see it before the colder weather sets in."

"Yes, there's not much of a growing season left, but it was good to do it this way. In this part of the state, the summer heat would stress new plants more than winter weather."

"You'll become the hottest new thing in landscape design, and everyone will fall over themselves to get you."

"Oh, fun," she answered lightly, even though Ben himself hadn't sounded pleased at the prospect. "I'll put up my rates."

"So when are you leaving?" he asked abruptly.

"Well…as soon as you want me to."

"We need to celebrate first."

"That would be good." Although he'd sounded as if it might be a mere duty for him. He rubbed at his lower stomach for a moment, wearing a strained expression, and she added, "What's wrong, Ben?"

"Nothing. Stomachache. It's fine. Will you stay till tomorrow, at least?" he said. "It's already, what, five o'clock? You can't go today."

"Come look through the garden, Ben," she blurted out. "I can't stand it that we're just hovering on the edge of the veranda like this." Talking and talking at each other. Not really saying anything. "Don't you want to see all of it? See if it matches the vision you had from the plans? We've done so much over the past couple of days, while you've been locked in meetings in the city."

The crew had worked until dark every day, and had begun again at seven each morning. Kate had brought refreshments and lunch out to them on laden trays, and had lingered to exclaim over the rapid changes. "It's gorgeous! Are there flowers I can pick for decorating the house, Rowena?"

"Yes, all of these beds here," Rowena had answered her. "I'll leave all the information you need about the best times to cut them, and how to encourage repeat blooming."

Ben stepped down from the veranda at last and they walked through the garden in an odd silence that Rowena didn't understand. Didn't he have questions? Was he waiting for her to point everything out? Or did he want to absorb it without speaking? Wasn't he happy?

She was so proud of it.

Proud of the kitchen garden laid out in patterns that reflected traditional motifs in Spanish mission architecture. Proud of the apricot and pomegranate trees, which with time would grow in espalier formation against a sunny wall. Proud of the citrus grove opening onto the swimming pool area, with its echo of the three-sided veranda that curved within the wings of the main house. Proud of the carefully selected cacti that she'd left in place, as a reminder of the jungle of desert vegetation that had been growing here just a few months ago.

"We definitely have to celebrate," Ben said at last, in the same tone in which people said about a boss they loathed, "We definitely have to give him a farewell party."

"So you like it?"

"Yes. Can't tell you how much, without sounding—" He stopped, pressed a fist into his stomach again, around where his belly button would be. Rowena didn't think he even noticed his own action. "And I hate doing that."

"Sounding…?"

"Yes."

He seemed to think that she knew what he meant.

Sounding emotional.

Sounding gushy.

Sounding insincere.

But she didn't know, really. He'd retreated to the Ben she remembered from weeks ago—from eight months ago, when she'd first come here—and from the second half of their horseback ride. The forbidding, distant Ben, with dark places inside him that he didn't want to share and demons he didn't want to admit to.

That Ben had never really gone away, she realized. It was always a part of him, but when things were sunny and smooth, it shrank or faded or something, and you could develop the dangerous illusion that it wasn't there.

"How?" she asked.

"How, what?"

"H-how do you want to celebrate? Have people here to look? Send out invitations? For some time on the weekend, maybe? To the gallery opening people, or your staff in the city, or—"

He swore. "No! Nothing like that. Throw a dinner, or something. A private dinner, tonight, not some huge, planned event. Just for us—you and me and Pablo and Wayne, their wives, and Kate. Except that doesn't work—making Kate cook when it's supposed to be a treat for her. I'd rather stay here."

"So get take-out pizza, a slab of beer and big tubs of ice cream," she suggested as a joke.

Men with assets that ran to eight figures, who hopped around in helicopters and got divorced by cool-headed wives because they weren't rich enough, didn't celebrate the completion of a major landscaping project with Wednesday-night pizza, ice cream and beer.

"I'm kidding, Ben," she added quickly.

"No, but it's perfect," he said. He laughed, and suddenly the other, sunnier Ben was back. "It's absolutely perfect."

And it was perfect.

For some reason, the idea energized him and he strode off to tell Pablo and Wayne that they and their wives were invited for pizza and beer at Santa Margarita tonight. He issued orders to Rowena over his shoulder as she followed him.

"Rowie, go tell Kate to stop cooking. Find out if she has take-out pizza menus anywhere. I'll get some beer up from the cellar. Have a look through the DVDs and pick a few options. There are a couple of things in there that might leap out at you, I think. Kind of appropriate. We'll watch a movie while we eat. And what's your favorite brand of ice cream?"

So the seven of them watched Helen Mirren in "Greenfingers," a British movie about gardening, redemption and romance, while sitting on Ben's handcrafted mahogany and leather sofas. They ate pizza with their fingers over paper plates, ready to catch any drooping strings of stretchy cheese, they drank beer direct from the bottle and they finished with scoops of Ben and Jerry's Cherry Garcia and Chocolate Fudge Brownie and Coffee Heath Bar Crunch.

It was such a friendly, homey kind of evening.

And then Pablo and Alicia and Wayne and Cindy went home, and Kate and Rowena dumped the mess of paper plates, crumpled napkins, beer bottles, pizza boxes, plastic spoons and sticky empty ice cream cartons in the kitchen. Kate went to bed, which made the living room very quiet apart from the sound of the DVD player clicking off, when Rowena went in there to say good-night to Ben.

At which point it wasn't friendly or homey anymore. This

wasn't Rowena's home. She was leaving tomorrow. And Ben was having problems, too.

"I can't do this," he said.

Can't do what?

Rowena looked the question rather than speaking it, because something about his tone made her scared to say the actual words. He was pacing through the room's expanse, more as if it was a prison than part of a beautiful and historic home. The enticing, down-home aromas of pizza and beer and ice cream still lingered in the air, and there were a couple of stray paper napkins that she and Kate had overlooked in their tidying.

"I can't let you go tomorrow…" he said, and did that rubbing action against his lower stomach that she'd noticed a couple of times today. She wondered what was bothering him.

Was it physical? He'd mentioned a stomachache.

Heaven knew, her own stomach didn't feel right, either. It was tied up in knots at the thought of saying goodbye to him. But she didn't dare to think that he was feeling the same way. He'd eaten too much pizza. Or he was developing the classic Type-A businessman's complaint—an ulcer.

She almost laughed at that idea. He wasn't that kind of man. He enjoyed too much about his life and didn't let it knot him up inside.

I'm the one doing that…

"…and mail a check for the final payment, and get Pablo to send you photos every six months. I can't, Rowena." He came closer and she stood her ground, watching him and resting her hand on the smooth leather back of a couch, not yet certain of what he wanted from her or what she could give.

Promises? He was the one who wasn't ready for those.

"Well, I did think you could manage to take your own photos," she murmured.

"I don't know what I am going to do, but I know I can't—" He stopped.

"There must be a choice," she said vaguely. He was such a commanding man, she could only think in terms of choices not impossibilities where he was concerned.

"There's no choice. Not tonight. Tonight I know exactly what I want."

So did Rowena now. Any possibility of ambiguity had vanished with his final step toward her. The friendship agreement was about to shatter like glass into a thousand pieces, and she would gladly pick up a hammer and deliver it the first blow.

But would shattering the friendship agreement be enough?

From Ben's face, he didn't think so.

"It's tomorrow where the problems start," he went on. "Tomorrow is when I won't be able to follow through on anything I say and do tonight. I want you in my bed so damn much, Rowena Madison, and I really care about you. I'd bend over backward not to hurt you. I'm not a man who doesn't know how to feel."

"I know. I think I know that better than you do."

"But there's no future I can give you. I'm trying to keep tomorrow in view, and not mess you around tonight, but I just can't. Not when you're leaving." He reached out his hand, but didn't touch her. "Not when I want you this much."

"So don't think about tomorrow, think about tonight." She took the hand, amazed at the contrast between its strength and its uncertainty, and laid it against her own cheek. Ben didn't move. Didn't caress her. Didn't take his hand away.

"You're not that kind of woman," he said.

"Let me be that kind." She moved their paired hands down to her shoulder and wrapped her free arm around his back. It felt achingly good to touch him, after weeks of holding back. The muscles in his back rippled beneath her touch and the solid bulk of his body seemed so precious. "Don't be so sure about what kind of woman I am. Let me decide that. Don't dictate my own soul to me."

"But I am sure. You're the kind who deserves more than I can give, and we've both known that all along."

"Maybe I'm changing."

"Changing into a woman who deserves less?" He swore. "Do you think I want you to change that way? Would I want you to become someone who can sleep with any man that takes her fancy and shrug it off the next day? Hell! That's the last thing I'd want!"

He squeezed the breath out of her suddenly, as if the fight with his own needs had made him clumsy. Then he rolled his forehead against hers, cupped his hands around her jaw and painted a short, hot kiss on her mouth. He whispered fiercely, "I'm sorry. I'm sorry. All of this is so impossible."

On both sides, their words began to run faster. More intense. More deeply felt. Clumsier. You grew clumsy when you talked this way, Rowena discovered. You grew so reckless in what you said and how you said it, and you didn't care. "I'm not talking about any man, Ben, I'm just talking about you."

"Which is a responsibility I can't take."

"Because I'm not strong enough?"

"I know you're strong. In surprising ways. But—"

"Not strong enough to deal with you. With this. That's such an insult, can't you see?"

"I think you're incredibly strong."

"Good!" She stretched her face up to reach his lips, desperate for his kiss, but he turned away from her mouth as if he couldn't take the risk.

"But that means your heart is strong, too," he said. "Your passions are strong. Your emotions. I can't match up to that. Not after the divorce."

"Leave those things to me, Ben. Leave me to work out for myself what I can take, and what I can't, and what you need to match up to. You're not responsible for everything."

"No?"

"I'll make my own decisions." But his shift in her arms told her he couldn't believe her.

They held each other in silence, Ben's breath warm on her neck and his body tight and still. "Could you take me making love to you tonight?" he whispered at last. "Is that really what you want?"

"I want it so much. Can't you feel it? Isn't every cell in my body telling you yes?"

"And then in the morning..."

"I know about mornings. They happen every day. They're a new start."

"The light is harsher."

"I can take the harsh light, Ben."

Still he didn't move.

"Do you know what would be the worst thing for me?" she said slowly.

"What, Rowie?"

"For you to patronize me. For you to decide, like some bossy...oh, medieval castle lord, or something...that it's up to you to call a halt, not me, because I don't know my own mind or my own weaknesses. For you to decide that you're responsible for my mistakes, instead of me taking the responsibility for them myself. Get over yourself, Ben Radford," she whispered. "Just...get over yourself. The whole universe doesn't stand or fall by what you can or can't do."

"Get over myself..."

"Yep. Now. Because I'm really losing patience waiting for you to make your move."

Would he?

She could hardly breathe, waiting to find out.

If he said no, she planned to keep pushing. If he walked her to her room like some nineteenth-century chaperone, told her good-night, and closed the door neatly between their fired-up bodies, she planned to creep back down the veranda in her bare feet to his wing of the house, climb into bed with him wearing nothing but skin and ravish him until he begged for mercy.

But she didn't have to do any of that.

"Here's my move, Rowie," he whispered. He laced his fingers through her loose hair and pulled her toward his waiting mouth.

There was something very different about the way they made love this time. The whole issue of control had completely gone. It didn't belong to Ben; it didn't belong to Rowena. It was shared or, more accurately, it just wasn't there.

Standing in the middle of the room, they pleasured each other with long, hungry, lavish kisses, going deeper, going everywhere. Clothing disappeared bit by bit, like a mutual striptease, each garment strewn in a mess on the living room floor. They stood naked, touching each other, not speaking.

Not daring to speak, Rowena knew, in case their words crossed the invisible line between clumsiness and cruelty.

Their bodies were so right together, so magical, but the rest was so tenuous. So much of it clashed. They wanted such different things. He was still protecting her too much, but she didn't have time or space to be angry about it. Not now. Not tonight. By shared and unworded agreement, they were banishing the clashes tonight.

"My room?" Ben asked.

"Yes."

Three words, that was all.

He led her there along the chilly corridor, pulled her against him in the doorway and warmed her with his big, hard body. He slid his fingers beneath her breasts and swooped down on her taut nipples with his mouth. He cupped her backside and brought her against his groin so she could feel exactly what this was doing to him.

His silky hardness pushed against her and she arched her back and pressed into him, swollen with need. He almost took her right there, and she wanted it. He lifted her onto his hips, and she wrapped her legs around him while he thrust into her, effortlessly carrying her weight, but then he whispered fiercely, "No, not like this. I want you on the bed. I want it to last."

They reached it and he pulled the covers back then held her again, his hands all over her almost roughly, as if he couldn't get enough of her, then gentling to whisper against her skin where it was most sensitive and most alive. He explored every inch of her body with his mouth as if he had to make a map of it in his memory.

The way I do with his body, she realized, because memories of Ben are all I'm going to have…

She let the thought go. Why think of loss, and spoil the sweetness of now?

Oh, now!

It was too much, and almost too good. She had to close her eyes and give herself to what he was doing because her senses were too overwhelmed to do anything but feel and take and react.

He pushed her back against the bed with her knees bent and her feet brushing the floor, and she didn't understand what he was going to do to her until it happened. The sweet touch of his tongue. It brought her to the brink so fast that the pleasure almost became pain and she twisted her whipping body away from him and dragged him up into her arms so she could cover his face in kisses while he plunged into her and kept her at the peak for endless dizzying seconds.

His size made her ache with fulfillment, and she held him so tight she could barely breathe. When he sank onto her, breathing hard, she cradled his head against her breasts, looking down at the dark hair spread over her soft skin, tickling the sensitized nipples that still throbbed from the wash of his mouth.

She felt him stir and draw in a breath. His voice was creaky when it came out. "You're wonderful, Rowie," he said. "I'm—" a moment's hesitation "—proud of you."

"That's an odd thing to say."

"No, it's not. It's just the truth."

"Okay."

They lay there for a long time, and she thought he'd fallen asleep but she wasn't sure. For herself, the steady breathing was a pretense. She didn't want him to talk or ask questions. She especially didn't want him to ask her if she was okay, because she didn't have an answer to that one.

Was she okay?

She knew that she loved him.

In her heart she'd known it for weeks, but it was the first time she'd let herself truly understand.

Funny, you know. It wasn't this huge, clanging realization, the way she'd expected it to be, all these years. It crept up on you slowly when you weren't looking and then suddenly it was there, already so familiar and so right. It shifted gradually like shadows with the movement of the sun, from chemistry and connection to something bone deep that you couldn't fully put into words.

And when you looked back and tried to pinpoint the moment, or even the day—the words he'd said, or the way he'd looked, or the deal-clinching shift in your own perception—you just didn't know.

You felt as if it had been there forever.

You'd loved him forever.

And you knew it was never going to stop.

Lying in his warm bed with his sleepy body flung all over her, Rowena felt as if she'd loved Ben Radford forever, and she had no idea if there was any kind of cure, or any kind of way through this that wouldn't hurt.

And still, against all logic, she wasn't sorry that it had happened, because it made her feel alive in a way she'd never felt before.

Chapter Fourteen

Slow and insistent, the pain dragged Ben out of sleep at around eleven o'clock.

It felt familiar, and he realized it was the same pain that had been nudging and nagging at him on and off all day. Previously, it had ebbed away just as he'd begun to focus on it, nudge at it with his fist and ask questions about it. He'd then forgotten it completely. After all, he was a busy man.

This time, however, it was stronger and it stayed. It was a pain that, frustratingly, he couldn't label. Too much dinner, for example. Or a stitch in his side. Nothing like that. It was…inexplicable. And it echoed the pain in his heart.

He lay beside Rowena, feeling the steady, innocent rhythm of her breathing as she slept, and tried to talk himself out of everything he was feeling. The sense of failure and loss that hovered over him because she was leaving tomorrow. The powerful urge to say all sorts of things to her that he knew he wasn't ready to say to any woman and didn't think he ever would be.

And finally, the pain in his gut.

Now *that* he could surely overcome by sheer force of will.

Because Ben Radford did not get sick.

When he had a cold, he sent an assistant out for some over-the-counter medication and kept going. When he had a headache...well, he just didn't have headaches. Maybe once a year. He couldn't remember the last time he'd known a day of real illness.

It was part of the Ben Radford mystique of infallibility, right alongside his ability to turn biochemical formulas into marketable products, his Midas touch with creative ideas and business enterprises, his attention to detail, and his gym-honed body.

So the pain would go, and he would get back to sleep, and in the morning...

In the morning Rowena Madison would leave, and he couldn't think of a single acceptable reason to make her stay.

In an ironic twist, his ex-wife was the person to provide him with the excuse to keep Rowie for just one more night. Heather called the next morning, while Ben was sitting on the couch in his office, in the middle of telling himself that a good breakfast and two cups of coffee would deal with the knot in his gut that seemed to be pulling ever tighter and harder.

"So I heard the garden is finished," Heather said on the phone, after the thinnest attempt at an innocent preamble.

"Yeah, who did you hear that from?"

"Oh, don't play games, Ben! You know perfectly well I heard it from Jennifer Sable, after her husband spent most of yesterday holed up in meetings with you."

"Well, there you go. Jennifer is right. So put her on permanent intelligence-gathering detail, if you want."

"You're not implying that this is none of my business, are you? You know I want to see what you're doing to the ranch."

"Why do I *know* it?"

"We did own it together once, remember?"

His stomach really hurt, and his body felt too warm, as if the pain was creating its own heat. He had to suppress a groan before he could answer. "Yes, Heather, we did, but we're divorced. We've split the DVD collection, the furniture and the bank account, and I'm not sure why you're still interested."

He could almost hear the offhand shrug down the phone line. She wasn't going to admit to her reasons. Maybe she didn't understand them herself. Ben thought it was her powerful competitive streak. She needed to believe—and prove to herself—that she was doing better for herself since the divorce than she would have done if they'd stayed together.

It was a little scary that he still understood her so well.

"Anyhow, so I'll be in the area this afternoon," she said, "and I thought I'd drop in and take a look, if that suits. Around four?"

"Sure." He'd be here. But he would make sure he had a conference call, or something, in order to avoid actually spending time with her. The easiest way to deal with the situation was to let Heather have her requested look at the garden and get it over with. "Pablo can show you around."

"I don't want Pablo, I want the doctor woman. Dr. Madison. Rowena. The one who's responsible for it."

"Thinking of hiring her to do your town house balconies?"

Heather's tone grew cagey. "A few people have been asking about her. I want to see for myself if she's any good before I lend my name to a recommendation."

"She's planning to drive back to Santa Barbara this morning, I think. I'm not sure that you'll be able to see her."

"Couldn't she stay just one more day?"

Bingo!

"It's in her interests, professionally," Heather went on, cajoling him coolly, as if she'd correctly guessed that he cared too much about Rowena's interests, professional and personal. "As you've implied, it could lead to more work."

Ouch, his stomach said, which wasn't a useful contribution to the conversation. "That's up to her," he managed.

"I'm sure you can persuade her, for my sake."

Resisting to ask why the hell he should do anything for Heather's sake, Ben made a noncommittal response and ended the call. Then he doubled up and sank into the couch with his knees pushed toward his chest, to see if he could squash the pain away.

He couldn't.

What the hell had he eaten yesterday?

"Listen, if you're interested in generating more clients in the San Diego area, you might want to stay an extra night," Ben told Rowena.

He'd sought her out in the dining room, where Kate was clucking around like a mother hen, attempting to feed her too much breakfast as usual—and on a day when she had no appetite at all. As soon as she'd awoken, showered and dressed this morning, she had begun to pack....

Ben hadn't eaten in the dining room himself, but he had a mug of coffee in his hand. He looked pale, and as if his thoughts were miles away. There was a disconnect between his attitude and his words. "You might want to stay an extra night," while his body language dug out a great big chasm of distance between them, and Rowena didn't have to ask him what was wrong, because she already knew.

She was leaving and he was terrified she'd get clingy and embarrass them both. She had no intention of getting clingy, but holding back might be the hardest thing she'd ever done in her life.

"Might I?" she answered him.

He gave an irritable shrug. "Maybe you have other commitments."

"I'd have to check."

"If you can stay, Heather wants you to show her around the garden." He read the surprise in her eyes and jumped in before she could speak. "I know. Since when do we have to accommodate my ex-wife?"

"That's not what I was—"

"Hey, it's okay if that was exactly what you were thinking. She can be demanding. In this case, though, there might be something in it for you. If she likes what she's sees, she'll talk about it."

"Okay. Thanks."

"Check your planner and let me know, will you? I'll need to call her back."

He wandered off, moving awkwardly. She had a horrible, blush-inducing thought that she'd whipped her body around so much in his arms last night she could have pulled a muscle in his back. Or was the awkwardness emotional rather than physical?

I'm leaving today.

It didn't feel real.

She gulped just enough breakfast to stop Kate from asking bossy questions about her appetite, and then retreated to her room to check her laptop planner. She could stay another night. Just one more. On Friday she had several appointments.

Kate handed over Heather's phone number with a grim expression. "Wash your ear out, afterward! Her venom can come right through the phone!" Rowena already knew that Kate wasn't a big fan of Ben's ex.

A brief phone conversation arranged a garden tour at four o'clock.

Ben emerged from his office long enough to ascertain that she was staying, then retreated again with a strained look on his face that told her he was unhappy but gave no hint of the cause. Rowena spent the next seven hours, with a lunch break in the middle, working on upcoming projects on her laptop in her room.

Heather appeared right on time. She was dressed down in the kind of smart-casual clothing that was never intended to get actual casual dirt on it, and she had her clever humor in place from the word go. "Project completed, then," she said, after they'd exchanged polite greetings.

"Well yes, but you haven't seen it yet. Come this way. This is my favorite way to see it, unfolding from the C-shape of the house. It's half-enclosed, and then it opens up, and—"

"Dr. Madison, it sounds wonderful and all very professional and beautifully conceived," Heather said slyly as they went out to the veranda, "but that's not the project I'm talking about."

Rowena looked at her blankly.

"I mean Ben's project, not yours."

"The garden is his, as much as it's mine. *More* than it's mine, of course," she corrected herself quickly, knowing that she had become far too emotionally invested in this place.

"I'm talking about what Ben's done with you." They stepped off the veranda together and Heather let the words sit for a moment, as if warming them nicely in the sun. Then she went on. "Your new confidence, your sparkle, your warmth blossoming forth."

"I…I don't know what you mean."

Another sly look. "Yes, you do. It's his magic touch. The Ben Radford touch. Turning things to gold." She looked at Rowena's hair, looped back in a high ponytail. "Look, even your hair, all those golden strands bleached in the sun, standing out against the brunette. Turned to gold, the way he always does. So symbolic!"

"Always?"

"Everything is a project to him, haven't you noticed? Radford Biotech, Radford Lateral Enterprises, the new gallery, the restaurant, this house. And now you. He takes something that interests him and works on it until it's perfect, and he never fails at it. I'll admit, I was more curious to see you than I was to see the garden, after what my friend Jennifer said about you as a work in progress."

"I...in progress?" Rowena was still a work in progress, as far as she was concerned. Listen to the familiar doubt kicking in, for example, under the onslaught of Heather's sly accusations.

"She came to dinner here, back in September," Ben's ex was saying. "You probably remember her."

And of course Rowena did. She remembered their conversation, too.

Ben's latest project.

"I thought she was talking about the garden."

"Well, that, too, of course." Heather smiled. "He never likes to work on just one thing at a time. And when the project is finished, he moves on. So let's take a proper look at it, shall we?" She walked ahead, exclaiming and praising, as if she hadn't just turned Rowena's whole world upside down.

Rowena followed, barely feeling the ground beneath her feet. It was lucky that Heather didn't seem to want a tour guide or botanical names, because she wasn't sure that she could have gotten the words out.

Ben's latest project.

She, Rowena, was one of his projects. He'd seen the possibilities, and he'd made improvements. He liked to see potential fulfilled. He didn't like failure or mistakes.

While she'd been kidding herself that she'd done all the work herself...

She remembered the way she'd been eight months ago, the day she first came here—proud of herself for managing one honest and rather heated conversation with a man like him. She remembered her first flight in the helicopter, her sensual appreciation of the clothes Rox had sent from Italy, the horse-back ride, the way Ben had put all the control into her own hands the first time they'd made love, and how good and necessary that had been.

Each new event had changed her a little, strengthened the confidence she'd been working so hard on for the past few years, given her a satisfaction that she'd hugged to herself and that she'd given herself numerous pats on the back for, never thinking about how much of it Ben could take the credit for.

And then last night she'd insisted to him how strong she was, and that she didn't need promises. She hadn't needed the security of control in his arms or in his bed, either. She'd been strong enough and certain enough to throw the control away.

She remembered the only words he'd spoken to her after-ward—words she'd intended to treasure, along with count-less memories of the time she'd spent at Ben's ranch.

You're wonderful, Rowie. I'm proud of you.

Project completed.

He'd virtually said it himself. He was proud of what he'd done.

And when the project is finished, Heather had said, *he moves on.*

Which he had told her he would do, all along.

Was he moving on, or…? There was another way to look at it, said a nagging voice inside her, but she didn't have time to think about that right now.

"It's wonderful," Heather said when they'd completed the tour.

"Which?" Rowena queried tartly. "The garden? Or the Madison project?"

Heather gave her a sharp, surprised look, then recovered

her humor and her cool. She grinned. "Oh, both, honey," she drawled. "I'm a huge, huge fan of both."

The rap at Ben's office door was sharp and loud and imperious.

Heather, he thought, and almost groaned as he pressed his hands on the desk to lever himself to his feet. The pain in his lower gut was still chewing away at him, and even though he'd stayed at his desk all day out of sheer stubbornness—he *never* got sick!—it hadn't gone away. He doubted that a conversation with his ex-wife, even if it was outwardly pleasant, would help.

But when he opened the door, it was Rowena standing there, not his ex.

"Where's Heather?" he said abruptly, aware that he couldn't even stand properly anymore. He had to tense up his stomach and lean forward at an angle, as if trying to dodge a low blow. The awkward posture made the pain only marginally less intense.

"She left."

"What did she think?"

"She thought your latest project had been a great success."

"So that's good, isn't it?" Through the fog of pain, he could see she seemed upset.

No. Not upset. Angry.

He didn't understand.

"She wasn't talking about the garden, Ben. She was talking about me."

"Well, you're responsible for the garden…" He was missing something here. And the pain in his gut was getting really vile now—still that dull ache beneath his navel, as well as a sharper pain on his right side. He felt queasy.

"Your project was me. You improved me. You worked on me. You *encouraged* me through all the things I was working on myself. Because that's what you do. You take something, and you have a vision for it, and you improve on it until it's—"

She stopped, blinked back tears and said in a hard, shaky voice, "I am so angry with you! And I guess you really have been successful with the Rowena Madison project, because I couldn't have said any of this to you a year ago. Not without crying and running. Which I am *not* going to do! I am so angry with you for turning me into a project, Ben Radford. For giving so much to me, when I thought I was giving it to myself. And you don't even value it enough to stick around. Value me. Heather says you move on. You don't. You run away. Only, you won't admit to that. Well, fine. I'm here to say goodbye, because my bags are in the car and I'm ready to go."

"I'm sorry," he said, between clenched teeth. Her words hadn't really sunk in. She was angry, okay, that was about all he got. Something about projects and value and sticking around. And he hadn't needed words to pick up on the state of her emotions. Her body language communicated those for her, loud and clear.

"Are you listening?" Rowena demanded suddenly. "Ben, are you okay?"

"I don't think so," he admitted, hating the words.

"What's wrong?"

"I think I need to get to the emergency room. Can you please call Kate?"

"Kate?"

"To drive me there."

Rowena gave him a rapid-fire questionnaire on his symptoms and his pain, and when she heard his answers, she told him, "There is no way Kate is driving you to the emergency room, Ben Radford." Her eyes still blazed. "If you're not going by ambulance, then you're going with me!"

* * *

They took Ben's Audi, with Rowena at the wheel. She'd mentioned the word *ambulance* again, but he wouldn't listen. "It's not going to be that serious," he insisted. "I've eaten something, or I've pulled a muscle."

"Maybe a denial muscle. You've certainly been giving those too much of a workout today. Or pretty much your entire adult life. And you were having some pain yesterday, weren't you?" She remembered his fist nudging at his lower stomach a couple of times, and his brief mention of a stomachache. "Why didn't you say?"

"Okay, not a pulled muscle," he said in a strained voice, "but we don't need an ambulance."

She didn't waste any more time arguing, because now that he'd admitted out loud to the pain, and admitted that it had taken hold last night or even earlier, it seemed to have built in him more strongly. His tanned skin had paled to a sickly green, and he felt feverish when she touched her palm to his forehead.

She couldn't bear to see him like this, when he was normally so strong. She had her theory about what was going on, but she wasn't going to share it with him because he probably wouldn't listen. She went to Kate in the kitchen, told her what was happening and promised to call with some news as soon as she could, then she grabbed Ben's car keys and helped him into the vehicle.

It was late on a Thursday afternoon, and the commuter traffic out of San Diego and Oceanside had just begun to build. Fortunately, Rowena and Ben weren't going in the same direction as most of the cars. She had forgotten her anger. It didn't matter while he was ill.

Rowena knew about illness, and about hospitals.

She felt herself going into the outwardly cool and practical but inwardly jittery state she remembered seeing in her parents all those times during her childhood. They'd made this same kind of journey numerous times—either a planned one, if she was scheduled for surgery, or an unplanned one. Several times the kind of simple cold that knocked Rox out for just a couple of days had progressed in Rowie's more fragile lungs to a dangerous chest infection.

Oh, yes, she most definitely knew about illness and hospitals!

"Tell me why you're angry," Ben croaked as they hit the highway.

"I'm not."

"Yes, you are. You were, just a few minutes ago."

"Do you really imagine I'm thinking about that now?"

"I want you to think about it. And to talk about it. What did Heather say to you that you've gotten so wrong?"

"I don't have it wrong. And that's only a part of it anyhow."

"Talk, Rowena. Don't play games."

"How can I talk now? How in the blue blazes are you in a position to listen to me now?" She gripped the wheel tighter and glared at him…and then she wanted to lean over and stroke the damp hair away from his pale, glistening forehead. How soon would he get seen, once they reached the ER?

"I'm listening," he insisted. "I'm not going anywhere."

"You're in pain."

"I can deal with it." He sat with his body hunched crookedly in the luxurious leather passenger seat of the Audi, suffering in a silence that said more about his physical state, in a man like him, than groans and complaints would have done. "I want to hear this, Rowie. If I have to have surgery today… I'm not getting knocked out and going under the knife with this hanging between us."

"We were about to say goodbye."

"And I've come up with a really inventive way to make you stay a little longer, haven't I?"

"Do you want me to stay longer?"

He was silent for a moment. "I don't want to let you go. I can't think beyond that."

"No, I don't suppose you can."

"For now, talk, please. Tell me what's going on."

"Heather congratulated me…congratulated *you,* really… on the success of your latest project. She meant me. The project was me. And she pointed to all the ways you like to see the potential in something and work on it and make it better. The biochemical research you turned into a major corporate success when you were still in grad school. All the beauty and attention to detail you've put into Santa Margarita. The gallery. And finally…me. And I don't want to be one of your projects, Ben."

"Don't buy into Heather's way of looking at things."

"In this case I do. Because it fits. All the ways you've pushed me and challenged me and then stood back smiling while you appreciated the successful transformation. Going horseback riding. Going up in a helicopter. Schmoozing with your wealthy associates and friends. And last night."

"Last night was *not* part of any project!" He let out a grunt of pain to punctuate the words.

"Last night I passed the final test. You even said it to me. 'I'm proud of you, Rowena.' Proud of your own handiwork. Because you love to succeed. Because everything you touch turns to gold."

"My marriage didn't. It went the other way. To dust."

"And you can't forgive yourself for it, can you? You're ashamed of it, because it was a project that failed. A great big mistake. Ben Radford's perfect record ruined by a nasty high-profile divorce. Which is making you run from anything that might give you the same kick in the guts. Well, I don't want to be a part of someone's perfect record. I don't want to have to measure up to a man who's ashamed anytime he fails. I don't want to entrust my heart to a man who's so scared of getting kicked in the guts. I love you, but I can't deal with any of that."

She had to blink back tears, and beside her, she heard another sound of pain—a tortured hiss of breath that made her put her foot harder on the gas pedal until the powerful European car flirted seriously with the speed limit and she expected to hear police sirens at any moment. She had to get him to the hospital.

"Keep talking, Rowie," he said, in a low, effortful voice. "I really want to hear this. Tell me it all. I need to know."

"I think you just need to close your eyes and rest now."

"No. Talk. I'm listening."

"If that's what you really want."

"Don't make me say it again."

"Okay, then." Out it came in a flood. "I can't deal with you being ashamed of failure, all right? Mistakes and failures are human, Ben. I've failed at a lot of things in my life. Sometimes I've even failed at walking out the door of my own apartment to go buy milk. I've stood on the stairs, heart pounding and hyperventilating, and then I've run back inside and felt shaky for the next half hour. And I'm *not* ashamed of that, anymore. It was a serious, clinical anxiety disorder, and I'm proud of myself for getting over it. But I know there are probably more failures ahead of me. No one gets through life without failing. You have to hold your head up."

She paused for breath, with a lot still left to say, since he seemed to want to hear it. He'd twisted toward her, the pain in his face warring with a different expression that her stolen sideways glances at him didn't give her time to read....

Then she saw the exit to the hospital flash by on her right. Shoot! She'd missed it.

Ben gave another groan beside her, as well as a sound that might have been an agonized laugh. "Hold your head up, Rowie, you missed the exit."

"I know. I'm sorry." She bit her lower lip. "I'm so sorry, when you're in so much pain."

"My fault." He laughed again. "I'm making you talk about stuff. It's kind of…a distraction. In a weird…difficult way."

"I'll take the next exit. There's a symbol for the hospital there, too, so there should be signs showing us the way. And if you're going to make me talk about stuff…my attitude to failure and success…how I feel about being your project… here's the Freudian connection—I won't pull over to the shoulder and tear up my driver's license just because of one missed exit, Ben. I'll keep driving until I get the route correct and arrive at the right place." She glanced sideways at him again. "And…and I'm really going to stop talking now, no matter what you say, because you're in too much pain to listen to any of this."

He had his hand over his face, shielding his grimace of pain, and this time he didn't argue.

They reached the hospital without further navigational errors a few minutes later. Rowena followed the signs to the ambulance entrance and pulled up as close to the emergency vehicle bay as she could without impinging on the clearly posted No Standing zone.

"Can you walk, Ben?"

"Of course I can!"

Yeah, right, with a knife prodding into his lower stomach at every step. Still, it was the quickest and easiest way to get him inside.

"I'll find the visitor lot and meet you at the triage desk," she told him.

"The where?"

"The ER. The front desk. The triage nurse will need to assess you, so they know whether to see you urgently, or whether you can wait. You'll find it. *Don't* downplay your symptoms, Ben, okay? The triage nurse needs you to be honest and accurate. Look, here's a paramedic, do you want me to—"

"I'll find it. I'll be fine."

Of course he would, Rowena thought. He'd be fine, with his teeth clenched, until it killed him. He'd die with the denial of any weakness still on his lips. He'd run away from the prospect of failure, never seeing that running away was the biggest failure of all.

Frustration tore at the lining of her stomach, mixed with other emotions she didn't want to name. Anger, and— Oh, what had she said to him just now? That she loved him? She hadn't meant to let it slip, but caught up in the current of powerfully felt words, the simple, elemental truth had flooded out all on its own, mixed up with everything she felt about Ben. Love, while seeing his flaws. Wanting, while knowing that she could never have.

She pulled out from the curb in a jerky rhythm that made the engine of the luxury car protest. Behind her, an ambulance siren sounded and she hurried to leave the emergency bay fully clear. Then she searched for the visitor parking lot, where she could only find a space right at the far reach of it. She gave herself a stitch in the side almost running back to the main hospital building.

Where she found Ben, downplaying his symptoms to the triage nurse, exactly as she'd told him not to do.

"It's okay, really," he was saying.

"And is it getting worse?"

"A bit, I guess, over the past hour."

"Any nausea or vomiting?"

"I haven't felt like eating. I think that's why I'm nauseous."

"I'll buzz you through and take your temperature. You do look pale."

"He looks green," Rowena said. "He's had serious pain in

his lower abdomen for nearly twenty-four hours, he's burning with fever and it's only getting worse."

The reason for the pain became apparent after a couple of examinations and tests. Ben had appendicitis—the diagnosis Rowena had guessed at but hadn't spoken to him out loud. The appendix had ruptured badly from the infection and the surgeons operated that night, removing the diseased organ, draining the peritoneal cavity and delivering a barrage of antibiotics, which they would continue through his IV for several days.

While Ben was in the OR, Rowena called the list of names he'd given her to let associates, family and friends in England and the U.S. know what was going on, and then she waited in the surgical family waiting room until the operation was over and his doctors came to tell her how it had gone.

"It was a mess in there," the senior surgeon said. "He's going to have a slow recovery. Why didn't he get medical attention sooner, do you know?"

"Don't worry, I'm going to hit him with that question before he's even out from under the anesthesia!" Rowena said.

Even though she already knew the answer.

Right now, aching with concern and care for him, she was angrier with him than she'd ever been with anyone in her life.

Chapter Fifteen

A millisecond after his last conscious moment on the operating table, Ben came slowly out from beneath the blanket of anesthesia feeling drunk and dry-mouthed and as if he'd been cut in half. He theorized that the woozy sensation in his head might lift a little if he opened his eyes, so he dragged his lids up.

The wooziness stayed the same.

But he saw Rowena.

He knew he couldn't keep his eyes open and manage to speak at the same time, so he closed the eyes again and said, "Hi."

"Hi, yourself."

Why was she still here? Maybe his appendix really had been swollen or something. He managed a shorthand version of the question. "Still here?" It was like speaking with a mouth full of cotton wads.

"I'm still here," she said softly, as if he was a baby.

He wanted to fight the idea. Him? A baby? In any sense? But the exact technique on the fighting thing was going to be a little tricky, given that he couldn't seem to move. His limbs were so heavy and soft, and...ouch!

"You have a button you can press when you need medication," she said.

What, and then the nurse comes? He had no idea.

He felt Rowena nudge the button device into his hand and position his thumb over the end of it. Her fingers were cool and soft, and her voice cooed like a dove. "Just press." He did so, and within seconds there came a sweet lessening of the knifelike feeling in his gut. He pressed again, but she told him, "It's set so it'll only deliver again after a timed pause."

Great. He was a baby, and his control was rationed by an electronic timer.

Rowena was still speaking, telling him in slow, simple and very controlled words what had happened, what the surgeon had said, how long he would probably be here, how he would feel tomorrow.

And tomorrow was when? What was today?

"Time?" he asked.

"About two in the morning."

"Which morning?"

"Friday. I mean, late, late Thursday night. The early hours."

He made some woolly-witted calculations. Early hours of Friday morning. About twenty-some hours since the pain had fully taken hold. Seventeen hours since Heather had called with her request to see the finished garden. Ten hours since Rowena had come hammering at his door, all angry and sizzling about what Heather had said. Nine hours and forty-five minutes since Rowie had told him in the car on the highway—still angry—that she loved him, and he'd been in too much pain to take it in or to respond.

Was she still angry now?

"You were lucky, Ben. If you'd ignored the pain much longer, you could have done serious damage to your insides."

She was still angry.

"But I didn't."

"You didn't. But you earned yourself a nice big incision instead of a couple of tiny holes. Because of the rupture, they couldn't keep the surgery to a laparoscopic procedure, they had to open you right up." Her voice shook. "Sometimes when they do that, when the damage is really bad, the scar tissue kinks up your guts and your system is never the same again. I could tell you about the girl in the next bed to me in the hospital when I was ten. She had a torn bowel that wouldn't heal, she was on intravenous feeding and she didn't get to eat real food for four months."

"You're telling me this because?"

"Because next time—"

"What next time?"

She didn't answer for a moment, then she said, "Okay."

"You're still angry."

"Yes."

"So tell me about next time."

"Next time you're wrong about something. Next time you fail. Next time your body lets you down, or you make a human mistake, or in some way the infallible Ben Radford golden touch comes up with lead instead of precious metal, maybe you'll realize that admitting up front to yourself that you *are* fallible can actually lessen the consequences and make things work out better. Running away from the hard stuff is not the power position, Ben."

His turn not to answer.

She loved him and she was angry with him, and here he was, too weak to open his eyes and talk at the same time, hanging out for when he could next press his pain button, knowing in his heart that she was right about a few things but not knowing where that left him, and none of it made sense.

The only thing that did make sense was that he needed Rowena to get out of his life, because he just couldn't deal with her seeing him the way he was now, and when he was better they'd be back to square one. He had nothing to promise and nothing to give, because if he and Heather could manage to fight their way through a divorce and come out still alive on the other side, he didn't think the same would apply to him and Rowena, and he could not bear the thought of risking such a thing, for a whole lot of reasons.

Now he just had to find a way to tell her.

Which turned out to be very simple, because the combined effects of anesthesia and pain didn't leave him with a subtle bone in his body. "Can you go? Can you…just leave?"

Silence.

"D'you hear?"

"Yes, Ben, I heard. Sure, I'll leave, if you really want me to."

"Please." In case there was still any doubt, he added, "Santa Barbara."

He waited for something more to happen, but nothing did. There came a tiny touch from her cool fingers against his hand, and the rustle of her movements, and then he was alone.

After a few hours of miserable sleep back at Ben's ranch, Rowena got ready to drive home to Santa Barbara.

She asked Kate about it over coffee in the kitchen at Santa Margarita, at the end of a heart-to-heart that had already lasted through two and a half cups. "Do you think I should stay?"

"If he told you to leave, you should leave." Kate raised her hands in a gesture that said Italian more than it said Irish. She clucked her tongue. "Let him find out for himself the hard way that the only thing he really wanted in this wide world today was for you to be there beside him in the hospital."

"You're a cruel woman, do you know that? I used to think you were really nice."

"Cruel to my boss when he deserves it this much! You're in love with the man, and if he can't see what that's worth—" Kate broke off and gave a snort.

Rowena didn't think she'd ever earned such an energetically supportive snort from someone before. Like a finger width of bandage over a six-inch paper cut, it helped, but not very much. The two of them packed an overnight bag of things for Ben—toiletries, books and magazines, a terry-cloth robe and some brand-new slippers Kate had bought him.

Rowena said an emotional goodbye to Kate and took the bag to the hospital at around ten, where she found he'd been moved out of the recovery suite and into a private room.

He was asleep.

When she tiptoed in, she found him there, lying in a sea of white hospital bed linen with his head sunk deep into a pillow, eyelashes dark on his cheeks and hand folded limply around his pain medication button. She put the overnight bag on the chair beside the bed and he didn't stir.

And I can't stay until he wakes up, she thought, because he's already sent me away once and nothing will have changed. He can't promise me a future because he knows it might fail and he's too scared of that, and I can't deal with living a life in which everything has to succeed or the world comes to an end. It doesn't! Life goes on.

In that spirit she crept out of his room and drove home to Santa Barbara, to get on with Day One of her Ben-free existence.

Recovering from a ruptured appendix, even in a luxurious private hospital room, was one of the most tedious experiences of Ben's life.

Repetitious rounds of medication and nursing checks. A truly horrible diet of clear soup, apple juice and jelly dessert. Visits from people who, with the exception of Kate, didn't know what to say. Kate, on the other hand, said far too much. He made a captive audience, and he knew that there was a serious seismic shift going on inside him when what she said started to make sense.

And then there were the physical therapy sessions in which he had goals like being able to get out of the bed and go sit in the chair, and being able to walk to the bathroom on his own.

What was more, they were goals he was very happy to achieve. Who would have thought that Ben Radford would ever flood with relief and satisfaction at the sheer fact of being able to take a normal morning shower or keep a bowl of yogurt down.

Now, who did that remind him of?

Rowena, of course.

Being able to buy a car without making fifteen visits to every dealership. Being able to leave her apartment to get milk.

Not that he needed reminders. He thought about her all the time, in a room crowded with elaborate flower arrangements ordered by friends and family and business associates from England and California and all over the U.S.A.

Most of the cards he hadn't even managed to read.

The thoughts were complicated, mixed up, impossible ones at first, but as his stomach muscles grew stronger and his pain lessened and his diet progressed to include real food, the thoughts grew simpler.

By the time he left the hospital on Tuesday morning, he knew what he wanted and what he was going to do. He didn't know if he had the slightest chance of success, but that whole failure-is-not-an-option thing sounded empty to him now. He'd learned that there were worse things than failure, and that the word *failure* itself had definitions he'd never dreamed of.

On Day One of her Ben-free life, Rowena sent him flowers. If this was a serious cheat on the Ben-free part, she couldn't help that. A major client currently in the hospital was owed the professional courtesy of flowers from Madison Garden Restorations, and since she was her own receptionist, courier and executive assistant, she had to arrange for the flowers herself.

On Days Two and Three, she didn't cheat and she was miserable. They'd been friends and lovers, and it felt so unfinished. She craved a better ending. She didn't *want* an ending at all, but to be left with one that had been so messy and cut into by the state of his hurting body and her own hurting heart made it even worse.

Day Four, she canceled her weekly appointment with Jeanette because she was too scared of what she might say. Three steps forward and two steps back. What was her next goal? Being able to get through a whole lifetime of Ben-free days.

Day Five, at around four in the afternoon, she cracked and picked up the phone.

"Kate, is he still in the hospital? How is he doing?"

"He's doing fine, eating properly and keeping everything down, healing nicely, and he came home this morning."

"I'm going to come down there. I can't stand it that we said goodbye to each other while he was out of his mind with pain and anesthesia. I'm going to drive down this afternoon, leaving in about five minutes. Would it be okay if—"

"Don't, darlin'," Kate said, cutting quickly across Rowena's words as if it might be dangerous to let her get to the end of the sentence. "Don't come down. Stay right where you are. What's the time?"

"Four o'clock. Well, ten after."

"Stay."

One word, spoken with a firmness that made it hard for Rowena even to manage a decent goodbye before she put down the phone. Kate thought the idea of coming down was *that* bad? She sat at her desk for fifteen minutes before she could gather her courage enough to open a computer file and start working on a project budget that needed to be done by the end of the week.

She'd got as far as calculating quantities of soil and mulch when the buzzer sounded at her outer office door.

Ben.

Oh, good grief, it was Ben.

He looked thinner and paler than he'd been this time last week, but he looked good, too. Boyish Ben, not forbidding Ben. The Ben who smiled when he challenged her and who looked at her as if she was beautiful. He looked *perfect.*

Shopping bags in his hands. Color in his cheeks. Words already on his lips before she could even say hello.

"Say everything to me that you said on Thursday, Rowena." He put the bags down and took her hands in his. "Say every word of it again, because I need to hear it. So much." He stroked the hair back from around her face, rolled his forehead across hers, and when she put her arms around him she felt him shaking.

"I...I can't." She was shaking, too. Her legs had gone weak. "I don't remember it anymore."

Blood was beating in her ears. The fact that he was here, the same day he'd come out of the hospital, had to be good...*didn't* it?...but she didn't know how good it was, yet, and she was too scared and too overwhelmed to try to guess.

"Kate told me...on the phone...not to come down," she said.

"When did you talk to Kate, sweetheart?"

"Just now. Twenty minutes ago."

"So this is why. Because she knew I was coming."

"I can't remember what I said to you last week. Any of it."

"So I'll have to say it instead." He swore under his breath. And then he didn't say anything at all, because he was kissing her as if he might never stop, and as if everything was already settled and solved and understood.

Which it wasn't, but Rowena couldn't manage to care when Ben had his arms around her like this. She held on to him like a shipwrecked sailor holding a floating spar, and the world made complete sense because he was here.

"Say it," she whispered at last. "I want to hear."

"I love you—can I say that first?"

"Only if it's true."

"Oh, hell, Rowena! It's true. I love you. I *love* you. I've had four days lying in the hospital finding out how true it is and finding out how right you were about everything you said."

"Not everything."

"No?"

"I told you I couldn't handle being in love with a man who can't deal with life's failures, but I've lived the alternative for the past four days, and that feels so much worse. I love you so much. That's all I can think about. That's all that matters."

"Let me say the rest. Please, sweetheart, because it's important." He kissed her again, and *that* was important. She had to fight to let him go.

"Okay, if it's important, I want to hear," she whispered at last.

"You know, when Heather came to take her look at our garden on Thursday, I knew exactly why she was there." He rubbed his cheek against hers, all warm and slightly rough, and then he looked at her. "Because she needed to check that she was still winning."

"Still winning?"

"She had to prove to herself that she hadn't made a

mistake, letting our marriage go. She had to deliver that dose of cattiness to you about you being my latest project in case she needed the extra edge."

"It felt *true* to me, though, when she said it."

"It's not true. I love watching you blossom. That's true. All the times you blossom. On Bonnie's back. In the helicopter. All the new things you discover about yourself that you love."

"You see—"

"But I'm not the one who makes it happen. I love it, but I'm not responsible for it. You do it on your own. I can read between the lines, Rowie. I can see what those heart operations did to your confidence, and I can see how far you've come since, purely because you've wanted to and you've worked at it and you've used all sorts of hidden strengths inside you. And I hope you never stop blossoming with the pleasure I see in you every time you discover something beautiful or do something new. You make me blossom."

"Yes? Really?"

"You make me over into someone I like a heck of a lot better than I liked myself before. If anyone is someone's project around here, it's me. I'm your project. And that project is never going to be completed. I like it too much. I love you too much."

"So what's the next step?" she whispered, and he kissed her again.

"I have to finish about Heather."

"I hoped maybe she was already finished."

"She's very nearly finished. You see, I realized that I understood her so well because we are...*were*...so alike in that. Competitive. Hating any suspicion of mistakes or failure. And it shook me up, because I can see what Heather has become because of it, and I don't want to be that way. I've never wanted to, and you're right. You're so right about all of that. In the hospital, oh hell..."

"Why did you send me away, when I wanted so much to take care of you?"

"Because I hadn't gotten to the point, then, when I could handle being taken care of. Boy, I soon learned! You know my first goal when the physical therapist came to my room? To learn the moves for getting out of bed."

"Oh, I remember those moves!"

"And I realized…you already know this…success and failure are so relative. So out of anyone's control. And so elastic. Getting out of bed can be a major success."

"Leaving your apartment to get milk."

"Learning to say, 'My divorce was the best thing that ever happened to me.'"

"That's a huge success," Rowena agreed.

"And making ten million dollars in a week can be a failure if you expected to make twenty, and if you have your priorities wrong. You don't know how sure of my priorities I am!"

"Will you tell me?"

"I'm telling you. All of this is telling you." His mouth closed over hers again, lingering until she began to melt all through. His priorities seemed pretty good, and Rowena explored them happily for a long time.

"Hey, I brought you a couple of things," he said softly.

He let her go and she wanted him back. She grabbed for his hand and they laced their fingers together while he reached for one of the shopping bags—blue and white plastic, with the words AC Pets and Aquariums printed on it.

"Ben?" She was laughing, happiness welling up inside her after what he'd said, as well as a giddy sense of mystery about what could possibly be in a pets and aquariums bag that was vital to give her right now.

Well, pet fish, of course.

Still laughing, totally confused, Rowena balanced the water-filled plastic bag in her hands while several seasick-looking neon tetras bobbed up and down. "They're—they are—"

"Bemusing you completely." He gave her another quick kiss. "You said the garden needed play places for kids, and I resisted that because there are so many mistakes you can make with kids. In fact, it's still a little scary to think about, so I'm hoping if we start with fish, we can move up to puppies and then…"

He reached for the second bag, made of black and gold paper, with braided gold satin handles and a curly, illegible logo on one side.

"Marry me, Rowena? Will you? So that when we're ready for kids in a couple of years they'll have two parents who are together and in love, who don't mind making a few mistakes, and who've had serious practice with puppies and fish?"

Rowena was still stuck on the word *marry,* never mind *kids, puppies* and *fish.* She couldn't speak.

Ben pulled a little black cardboard box out of the bag. Inside the cardboard box was a velvet box, and inside the velvet box was a diamond ring that made her gasp and brought tears to her eyes.

"This is just the practice ring, too, not the real one. Say yes, would you? I'm so hoping you're going to say yes—so I can put it on."

"Yes, oh, yes."

"Very, very nice answer." He kissed her.

Kissed the hand with the ring sparkling freshly on one finger. Kissed her neck below her ear and whispered his love again. Kissed her mouth until she could barely breathe. She had the bag of tropical fish still in her hand and it squished against them, providing one of those little flourishes of imperfection that they both knew, now, were so important.

Kissing and fish.

Somehow it worked.

"We'll buy a better one later on," he said about the ring.

"This one looks pretty good to me."

"Yeah, but I want us to choose the right ring together. Because you have a little thing with control, sometimes, beautiful Rowie. You don't like me to make all the moves."

"You're making them right now..."

"Is that okay?"

"Oh, yes..." Some minutes later she finally got around to asking him, "What's in the third bag?" It was a big, sturdy one made of strong white paper, and it looked heavy and full, sitting there on the floor.

"A picnic from Kate."

"Mmm, tiny food."

"Because she thought you might take me to your apartment, and that we might not want to go out tonight, since I'm a convalescent surgical patient and all."

"How did you even get here? You didn't drive?"

"Helicopter and limo. I'm not allowed to drive yet. And I didn't bring any spare clothes."

"I'm envisaging that you won't need many clothes for tonight."

"I'm envisaging that you'll have to be very, very gentle with me."

"That could be fun."

He got serious suddenly. "Because it's you. It'll be fun because it's you, Rowena. It seems so simple now."

"Yes?"

"Just you and me, and everything else falls into place."

And that night and beyond, everything did.

Epilogue

Ben heard splashing.

The helicopter had risen into the air to head back to San Diego, and as the sound of the rotor blades faded, they were overtaken by the sound of splashing, which drifted to his ears across the adobe wall that masked the pool from view on this side of the house.

Oh, and what were those other sounds? Laughing and shrieking and something else he couldn't make out, something excitable and loud, drowned out this time by an enormous splashing sound.

They're still in the water, he thought happily, and loped quickly into the house to change out of his business suit. He was clumsy with impatience as he climbed into baggy blue swim shorts and grabbed a towel. He wasn't going to miss the sight this time around....

Yes!

Coming through the lush, beautiful courtyard section of the garden, through the kitchen garden, green with spring lettuces and herbs, and finally through the fragrant wash of orange blossom that hovered all through the citrus grove, he saw Rowena first. She wore a scarlet bikini that made her look like one hot mama, and in her arms she held eleven-month-old Will. The May sunshine sparkled on the pool's blue water and the air was hot and dry.

It was Will's second swim in the pool at Santa Margarita. Ben had missed the first one—he'd been in Los Angeles on business—and he didn't intend to miss this one, too. He'd thought so hard about having children. They'd waited two years before trying for a baby. He wanted to be the right kind of father, in every way he could. Most of all, he wanted to be there. Just be there, for Rowena and Will and the second baby already on the way.

But he didn't want his wife and baby son to realize just yet that he was here, watching them. Rowie must have heard the helicopter, but she wouldn't be expecting him to get out to the pool in his swim shorts this fast. He loved taking these brief snatches of time to watch them when they were unself-conscious and unaware.

Rowena lifted Will up to the edge of the pool. He was walking already, had been for nearly a month, with rapid, tottering steps that brought him within reach of trouble in about two seconds flat. Now he stood on the pale tiles and reached out his arms to her and she told him, "Jump, Will! Jump to Mommy!"

But he didn't. Not right away. He just stood there laughing down at her while she held out her arms, waiting for him.

Ben came forward. They still hadn't seen him.

Which meant he was only a few feet away when he distinctly heard that other sound he hadn't identified as he'd approached the house.

"Mommeemommeemommee!"

Will's very first word.

"Yes, jump to Mommy!" Rowena said, and then she must have seen something out of the corner of her eye, because she turned and saw Ben, just as Will landed in the water and in her arms with another enormous splash.

"He said Mommy. Oh, wow! Oh, *wow!*"

Rowena grinned. "I know. First time. Just since we've been in the pool. Oh, I'm so glad you're home early!"

"So am I…" He slid into the water and reached her in seconds to plant a lingering kiss on her sweet, cool mouth.

"I guess because he loves jumping in," Rowena said, "and I've been saying, 'Come to Mommy' each time while he's standing on the edge, and suddenly he was just saying it, every time he jumped. Mommy, Mommy, Mommy." She was laughing, thrilled at the milestone.

Ben was thrilled, too. Will turned to him and held out his arms and Rowena passed him across. They had a big, cool, very wet hug and, after a long two days of meetings, Ben's world was right again.

Almost right.

He hadn't realized that it was possible for it to get even *more* right…perfect…but seconds later, it did.

Rowena took Will again and lifted him back onto the edge of the pool for another leap into the water. He stood there with water running down his legs, his face lit up, his arms stretched out and his whole body getting ready to spring. Then he turned just a little and changed the direction of his mighty launch into the water.

"Daddydaddydaddy!" he said as he leaped, and Ben really knew that he was doing this right in all the ways that mattered.

* * * * *

THOROUGHBRED LEGACY
*The stakes are high when it comes to love,
horse racing, family secrets
and broken promises.*

*A new exciting Harlequin continuity series coming soon!
Led by* New York Times *bestselling author Elizabeth Bevarly*
FLIRTING WITH TROUBLE

Here's a preview!

THE DOOR CLOSED behind them, throwing them into darkness and leaving them utterly alone. And the next thing Daniel knew, he heard himself saying, "Marnie, I'm sorry about the way things turned out in Del Mar."

She said nothing at first, only strode across the room and stared out the window beside him. Although he couldn't see her well in the darkness—he still hadn't switched on a light...but then, neither had she—he imagined her expression was a little preoccupied, a little anxious, a little confused.

Finally, very softly, she said, "Are you?"

He nodded, then, worried she wouldn't be able to see the gesture, added, "Yeah. I am. I should have said goodbye to you."

"Yes, you should have."

Actually, he thought, there were a lot of things he should have done in Del Mar. He'd had *a lot* riding on the Pacific

Classic, and even more on his entry, Little Joe, but after meeting Marnie, the Pacific Classic had been the last thing on Daniel's mind. His loss at Del Mar had pretty much ended his career before it had even begun, and he'd had to start all over again, rebuilding from nothing.

He simply had not then and did not now have room in his life for a woman as potent as Marnie Roberts. He was a horseman first and foremost. From the time he was a school-boy, he'd known what he wanted to do with his life—be the best possible trainer he could be.

He had to make sure Marnie understood—and he understood, too—why things had ended the way they had eight years ago. He just wished he could find the words to do that. Hell, he wished he could find the *thoughts* to do that.

"You made me forget things, Marnie, things that I really needed to remember. And that scared the hell out of me. Little Joe should have won the Classic. He was by far the best horse entered in that race. But I didn't give him the attention he needed and deserved that week, because all I could think about was you. Hell, when I woke up that morning all I wanted to do was lie there and look at you, and then wake you up and make love to you again. If I hadn't left when I did— the way I did—I might still be lying there in that bed with you, thinking about nothing else."

"And would that be so terrible?" she asked.

"Of course not," he told her. "But that wasn't why I was in Del Mar," he repeated. "I was in Del Mar to win a race. That was my job. And my work was the most important thing to me."

She said nothing for a moment, only studied his face in the darkness as if looking for the answer to a very important question. Finally she asked, "And what's the most important thing to you now, Daniel?"

Wasn't the answer to that obvious? "My work," he answered automatically.

She nodded slowly. "Of course," she said softly. "That is, after all, what you do best."

Her comment, too, puzzled him. She made it sound as if being good at what he did was a bad thing.

She bit her lip thoughtfully, her eyes fixed on his, glimmering in the scant moonlight that was filtering through the window. And damned if Daniel didn't find himself wanting to pull her into his arms and kiss her. But as much as it might have felt as if no time had passed since Del Mar, there were eight years between now and then. And eight years was a long time in the best of circumstances. For Daniel and Marnie, it was virtually a lifetime.

So Daniel turned and started for the door, then halted. He couldn't just walk away and leave things as they were, unsettled. He'd done that eight years ago and regretted it.

"It *was* good to see you again, Marnie," he said softly. And since he was being honest, he added, "I hope we see each other again."

She didn't say anything in response, only stood silhouetted against the window with her arms wrapped around her in a way that made him wonder whether she was doing it because she was cold, or if she just needed something—someone—to hold on to. In either case, Daniel understood. There was an emptiness clinging to him that he suspected would be there for a long time.

* * * * *

THOROUGHBRED LEGACY
Coming soon wherever books are sold!

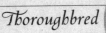

Thoroughbred *Legacy*

Launching in June 2008

A dramatic new 12-book continuity that embodies the American Dream.

Meet the Prestons, owners of Quest Stables, a successful horse-racing and breeding empire. But the lives, loves and reputations of this hardworking family are put at risk when a breeding scandal unfolds.

Flirting with Trouble

by *New York Times* bestselling author

ELIZABETH BEVARLY

Eight years ago, publicist Marnie Roberts spent seven days of bliss with Australian horse trainer Daniel Whittleson. But just as quickly, he disappeared. Now Marnie is heading to Australia to finally confront the man she's never been able to forget.

The stakes are high when it comes to love, horse racing, family secrets and broken promises.

A new exciting Harlequin continuity series coming soon!

Royal Seductions

Michelle Celmer delivers a powerful miniseries in
Royal Seductions; where two brothers fight for the
crown and discover love. In *The King's Convenient Bride*,
the king discovers his marriage of convenience to the
woman he's been promised to wed is turning all too
real. The playboy prince proposes a mock engagement
to defuse rumors circulating about him and restore
order to the kingdom...until his pretend fiancée
becomes pregnant in *The Illegitimate Prince's Baby*.

Look for

THE KING'S CONVENIENT BRIDE
&
THE ILLEGITIMATE PRINCE'S BABY

BY MICHELLE CELMER

Available in June 2008 wherever you buy books.

Always Powerful, Passionate and Provocative.

REQUEST YOUR FREE BOOKS!
2 FREE NOVELS PLUS 2 FREE GIFTS!

SPECIAL EDITION®
Life, Love and Family!

YES! Please send me 2 FREE Silhouette Speáal Edition® novels and my 2 FREE gifts (gifts are worth about $10). After receiving them, if I don't wish to receive any more books, I can return the shipping statement marked "cancel." If I don't cancel, I will receive 6 brand-new novels every month and be billed just $4.24 per book in the U.S. or $4.99 per book in Canada, plus 25¢ shipping and handling per book and applicable taxes, if any*. That's a savings of at least 15% off the cover price! I understand that accepting the 2 free books and gifts places me under no obligation to buy anything. I can always return a shipment and cancel at any time. Even if I never buy another book from Silhouette, the two free books and gifts are mine to keep forever.

235 SDN EEYU 335 SDN EEY6

Name	(PLEASE PRINT)	
Address		Apt. #
City	State/Prov.	Zip/Postal Code

Signature (if under 18, a parent or guardian must sign)

Mail to the **Silhouette Reader Service:**
IN U.S.A.: P.O. Box 1867, Buffalo, NY 14240-1867
IN CANADA: P.O. Box 609, Fort Erie, Ontario L2A 5X3

Not valid to current subscribers of Silhouette Speáal Edition books.

Want to try two free books from another line?
Call 1-800-873-8635 or visit www.morefreebooks.com.

* Terms and prices subject to change without notice. N.Y. residents add applicable sales tax. Canadian residents will be charged applicable provináal taxes and GST. This offer is limited to one order per household. All orders subject to approval. Credit or debit balances in a customer's account(s) may be offset by any other outstanding balance owed by or to the customer. Please allow 4 to 6 weeks for delivery. Offer available while quantities last.

Your Privacy: Silhouette is committed to protecting your privacy. Our Privacy Policy is available online at www.eHarlequin.com or upon request from the Reader Service. From time to time we make our lists of customers available to reputable third parties who may have a product or service of interest to you. If you would prefer we not share your name and address, please check here. ☐

Silhouette®

Romantic
SUSPENSE

Sparked by Danger,
Fueled by Passion.

Seduction Summer:
Seduction in the sand…and a killer on the beach.

Silhouette Romantic Suspense invites you to the hottest
summer yet with three connected stories from some
of our steamiest storytellers! Get ready for…

Killer Temptation

by Nina Bruhns;

a millionaire this tempting is worth a little danger.

Killer Passion

by Sheri WhiteFeather;

an FBI profiler's forbidden passion incites a
killer's rage,

and

Killer Affair

by Cindy Dees;

this affair with a mystery man is to die for.

Look for

KILLER TEMPTATION by Nina Bruhns in June 2008
KILLER PASSION by Sheri WhiteFeather in July 2008
and
KILLER AFFAIR by Cindy Dees in August 2008.

Available wherever you buy books!

Visit Silhouette Books at www.eHarlequin.com   SRS27586

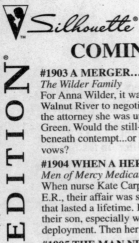

COMING NEXT MONTH

#1903 A MERGER…OR MARRIAGE?—RaeAnne Thayne
The Wilder Family
For Anna Wilder, it was double jeopardy—not only was she back in
Walnut River to negotiate a hospital takeover her family opposed,
the attorney she was up against was long-ago love interest Richard
Green. Would the still-tempting single dad deem Anna a turncoat
beneath contempt…or would their merger talks lead to marriage
vows?

#1904 WHEN A HERO COMES ALONG—Teresa Southwick
Men of Mercy Medical
When nurse Kate Carpenter met helicopter pilot Joe Morgan in the
E.R., their affair was short but very sweet…and it had consequences
that lasted a lifetime. Kate had no illusions that Joe would help raise
their son, especially when he hit a rough patch during an overseas
deployment. Then her hero came along and surprised her.

#1905 THE MAN NEXT DOOR—Gina Wilkins
Legal assistant Dani Madison had learned her lesson about men the
hard way. Or so she thought. Because her irresistible new neighbor,
FBI agent Teague Carson, was about to show her that playing it safe
would only take her so far….

#1906 THE SECOND-CHANCE GROOM—Crystal Green
The Suds Club
When the fire went out of his marriage, firefighter Travis Webb
had to rescue the one-of-a-kind bond he had with his wife,
Mei Chang Webb, and their daughter, Isobel, before it was too late.
Renewing their vows in a very special ceremony seemed like a good
first step in his race for a second chance.

#1907 IN LOVE WITH THE BRONC RIDER—Judy Duarte
The Texas Homecoming
Laid up after a car crash had taken all that was dear to him, rodeo
cowboy Matt Clayton was understandably surly. But maid-with-a-
past Tori McKenzie wasn't having it, and took every opportunity to
get the bronc rider back in the saddle…and falling for Tori in a big
way!

#1908 THE DADDY PLAN—Karen Rose Smith
Dads in Progress
It was a big gamble for Corrie Edwards to ask her boss, veterinarian
Sam Barclay, if he'd be the sperm donor so she could have a baby.
But never in her wildest dreams would she expect skeptical Sam's
next move—throwing his heart in the bargain….

SSECNM0508